Totally Bound Publishing books by SA Welsh:

Out of CTRL

I0570385

OUT OF CTRL

SA WELSH

Out of CTRL
ISBN # 978-1-78430-306-8
©Copyright SA Welsh 2014
Cover Art by Posh Gosh ©Copyright October 2014
Interior text design by Claire Siemaszkiewicz
Totally Bound Publishing

OUT OF CTRL

Dedication

For Mum.

Special thanks to Faith, for making sense of the madness.

Chapter One

"Are you coming home for Dad's sixtieth?" Andrew Finley's eldest sister Sara nagged down the phone line. His family had hounded him constantly for two weeks. Why couldn't his relatives take the hint or act like a normal family and avoid each other?

"I told you, Sara, I don't know if I can get the time off —" Something told him this wasn't going to be as easy as he'd hoped.

"Andrew Norman Finley! Don't you dare try to feed me that line of crap again. The first time I let it go, but no more. If you don't come, I'll tell Mom why," Sara threatened.

Sara and her boyfriend Steve, and his other sister Jenifer-Annie — Genie for short — came for a visit every few months and stayed a week, and they talked often enough in between. Why couldn't they just continue doing that?

"I don't know what you mean…"

She might let it go. Nope. His luck just wasn't that good.

"Cut it out, little brother. This is because of Teddy, isn't it?"

Even hearing the man's name made him catch his breath, sit back in his chair then push away from the desk. There was no way he could deal with physically seeing *him*.

What could he say to that?

"Angela's boyfriend is none of my concern," he replied coldly.

This was a dangerous subject for him and he wasn't about to spill his guts to anyone. Not even his overprotective big sister.

"Don't even bring that little trollop into it, Andrew. It's not what you think. They're not together. They never were, really." She sighed.

But Andrew wasn't listening.

He was successful, in his own way. He'd made a name for himself in computer coding and encryption programing. And nothing was going to make him turn back into his former self.

Nothing. Especially not that town.

Christmas and Thanksgiving were fine. There was no pressure and he could come and go as he pleased as long as he rang. So he chose not to go at all and just dropped them a holiday message when he knew the family would be too busy to answer the phone.

Genie and Sara came a few weeks a year and he admittedly loved spending time with them but he never returned the favor. He never went home. Not since he'd left for college nine years ago.

"You have *no idea*, Sara, so just drop it."

"Andrew. Drew, I didn't mean to—" Sara desperately tried to backpedal but it was too late.

Usually she backed off long before now.

Pinching the bridge of his nose, Andrew let out a harsh breath. "It's fine. Just don't go there, okay? Why is this so important to you, Sara?"

"I can't tell you but I really need you to be home this weekend. Please, for me and Steve?"

So they were on to the emotional blackmail part of the conversation.

"We need you here for this," she pressed.

"Enough. I'll come *if* I can but if Angela comes near me then—"

He felt guilty enough for not wanting to go to his dad's sixtieth birthday, even though he wasn't close with his parents. But his mother had sounded so tired the last time she'd called him and that played on his mind.

"Then I'll sic Mom on her. I'll tell her the reason the nice Robinson couple down the street had a 'difference of opinion'. Mom loves Mrs Robinson and will be out for blood if she finds out the family slut was the one to break up a happy home."

"Come on, it couldn't have been that happy—" he started.

He'd seen too many friends go through hell after their other halves had cheated on them. Some had even been the cheater but most of the time there had always been underlying problems in the relationship. Either that or the cheater was just a rat bastard—male and female alike.

In his mind, there was no excuse for cheating.

If you wanted someone else enough to risk what you had at home then you needed to be honest. Make a decision and have enough respect for the person you're with not to betray them.

But then he'd never actually been in a relationship, so what did he know? Maybe it was more complicated than that. Andrew picked at a piece of lint on his trouser leg as he thought about his love life.

There had been a few dates here and there over the years but no one special. There was no risk of being hurt if a person didn't care to begin with. That's what he told himself anyway.

"No, really, they were happy," Sara assured him. "Angela got him drunk and slipped him something. I heard her talking about it with the bimbo twins. The man was so distraught after it wore off that he packed up and left the city. He was a good guy."

"Holy shit. That's date rape, Sara," Andrew was at a loss as to what else to say.

He fiddled with his glasses, bouncing the frames on his nose. The forth bounce had him snatching his hand down. He'd worked too hard for old habits to resurface now.

"I know. I'm trying to track him down and see if he wants to press charges. If he does, then I'll report to the police as a witness to a confession. I taped the bitch on my phone too but I don't want to do anything without speaking to Mr Robinson first." Sara seemed outraged that someone would do such a thing. In fact, his sister sounded disgusted but determined nonetheless.

"Again I repeat—holy shit. Are you any closer to finding him yet?"

"No. I can't find him but I'm going to keep trying." Sara sighed.

Andrew realized just how much this was affecting his big sister.

"Email me whatever information you have on him. Friends, family, where he used to work, everything, and I'll see if I can help." Hell, he could probably track the man down simply from his name alone but his sister didn't need to know that. Andrew just didn't want to answer the questions that would follow if he did. After all, his family still thought he worked as an IT tech for some admin company. And that was the way he wanted it to stay for now.

In reality, he worked as a freelance hacker or rather a reformed hacker who now only hacked for the 'good' guys. At least that's what he told himself. There was some shady information he came across on the job sometimes but it wasn't his place to judge the CIA's actions.

Just because he wasn't the moral police didn't mean he wasn't storing information away in case there came a time he could do something about it. Some of the stuff gave him nightmares. Well, *more* nightmares. He had feelers out searching for anyone who was high enough up the food chain to take action but wasn't corrupt as well.

It was an unsurprisingly hard task.

"You can help? But I thought you only fixed computers and stuff." She obviously realized how disbelieving she sounded and Andrew almost smiled when his sister started backpedaling again.

"I... I mean great. Any help you could give me would be awesome," Sara gushed before pausing to see if he'd take the olive branch.

"No problem. I think you'd be surprised at what I can do with my computer, sis," he teased, for once enjoying the secret that was his life. Sara wasn't stupid by any means, so he would probably have an inquisition in his near future.

"Okay, little brother. Thank you but don't think you're getting away with being evasive for long. Love you."

With that, she hung up leaving Andrew smiling. At least until he remembered why she'd called in the first place.

The severity of the situation dawned on him.

He had to go home.

The noise of his phone handset smashing against the wall wasn't nearly as satisfying as he wanted it to be.

* * * *

Andrew stomped on the welcome rug to knock the dirt from his boots before slamming the door to his large two-bedroom apartment closed. The heavy door made quite a nice thwack and he only felt a little guilty that he might disturb his neighbors.

Only a *little* guilty, though. His neighbors weren't that nice and he was pretty sure one of them was following him and spying on him for Andrew's boss.

He threw his keys into the glass bowl on the counter. Andrew walked past the kitchen and into the sizeable living area where he set his laptop on the glass coffee table.

This little beauty was a work of art, if he did say so himself. The second a digital device touched the table surface or came within a foot of it, the tiny computer-bots he'd created started to download the information on that device.

The information was stored under multilayer encryption he'd written himself then he sent it to two secret portable hard drives he kept in safety deposit boxes at train stations on opposite sides of the state.

Andrew guessed he might be paranoid but when working with the CIA—and not entirely willingly—one could never be too paranoid.

It only took a few seconds for the information transfer to complete. Falling into the beat-up chair, he sighed and closed his eyes.

What a hell of a day.

Between his sister calling, tracking down Mr Robinson and explaining what Sara had overheard, then doing his actual job, he was exhausted.

Tracing funds related to terrorist organizations and following the money to a secret bunkers and bank rollers was harder than it sounded, and he was certain he'd worked twenty hours straight on that alone.

Lifting his wrist, he squinted at his watch. Yep. It had been too fucking long since he'd had a break. Perhaps going home wasn't the worst idea in the world after all. It was definitely top three but at least he'd have his mother's cooking and a break from work. Being isolated from the city could give him time and freedom to sift through the information he had on his boss as well.

Would it really be worth it?

Probably not.

But it did mean he'd get to see Genie's new restaurant.

Digging his cell phone out of his pocket before he changed his mind, he shot off an email to his boss saying he was taking the weekend for himself and going off grid.

Off grid meant he didn't want to be contacted unless aliens descended. Okay maybe not aliens but there had to be a definite threat of impeding Armageddon unless his boss wanted to be flooded with Viagra and penis enlargement spam ads for the foreseeable future.

Amazing how fast word spread when you did that to an asshole agent, who took the fact that he had a badge as a license to bully everyone he considered to be under him. A few little pop-up bombs to set off a flurry of porn sites, to take over the home screen every time the computer booted up, was kid's play.

The bastard couldn't prove he'd done it, though.

And as it had turned out, the guy's higher-ups hadn't liked his boss either, so the case had never gone any further than the asshole shouting at him. Andrew had even received a gift basket from the man's co-workers.

Smiling at the memory, Andrew dragged himself onto to his feet and stumbled tiredly into the master bedroom, undressing as he went. In only his underwear, he entered the attached bathroom and started the water running.

"God, I really need a hot bath," he moaned as he stretched the cramping muscles in his neck and back.

This was one luxury he'd let himself splurge on.

He had a glass-walled shower with the largest showerhead he could find sitting in one half of the bathroom and a separate claw-foot bathtub in the other. He dimmed the lights to a slightly less offensive brightness and stripped off his boxers before getting into the steaming tub.

As soon as he sank into the warm welcome of water, he could almost feel the day's stress starting to leave him. Andrew removed his glasses before carefully putting them on the glass shelf behind him.

Sinking in the water so it sloshed over his shoulders, he took a breath and submerged completely. This tub was old-fashioned but the perfect size for his five-foot-ten-inch frame, allowing him to slip under the water and not spill the contents all over the floor.

There was just something about being underwater that was peaceful. Everything was silent. Calm. Like the outside world couldn't touch him.

Sooner or later, he had to come back up, though. He winced as the water and bubbles ran into his eyes. Even though the soapsuds stung like a bitch, he seemed far less stressed than when he'd first come home to his apartment.

Home.

The day he'd packed up his stuff and started for college, he'd sworn he'd never go back to a town full of busybodies and assholes. If he ever saw most of them again, it would be too soon. He especially never wanted to see Angela.

The Omen child had nothing on his sister. She was evil to the core but for some reason or another, their parents had always been blind to it. Every time she'd screwed up, or had screwed someone up, his mother had believed whatever lies Angela told.

Sometimes he thought his father might see his daughter for the person she really was but he never spoke up, just shook his head and hid behind his newspaper.

What had happened with Mr Robinson was going to break his mother's heart.

Perhaps it might be the step his parents needed to knock them back into reality. It might seem harsh but he wasn't feeling particularly generous after a lifetime of hell at Angela's hands.

Sara didn't know the worst of it, didn't know what had happened the night he'd decided to pack up and leave town for early college admission.

Not even the hot water could stop his shivering or the stabbing cold that pierced him at the memory. Getting out of the bath, he pulled the plug and went to stand in front of the large mirror that covered most of the far wall.

When the builder had originally suggested it for light, because the room didn't have a window and artificial light hurt his eyes after a while, he'd thought it was a good idea. But now, standing naked and seeing his pale, thin body staring mockingly back at him, he wanted to smash the thing into a million pieces.

The only thing that held him back was the seven-year bad luck superstition his mother had always believed in. He couldn't afford to risk it. Andrew had enough bad luck for three people as it was.

In high school, he had been the clumsy nerd with a stutter who wore spotty Coke-bottle glasses. And now he was still all of those things except coated in a layer of designer glasses and he was borderline OCD. He kept highlights in his chestnut hair and he had enough money in the bank to last him the rest of his life if he needed it to.

He was a success. So why didn't he feel like it and why did he let his family think he was just another grunt on the ladder? Why couldn't he be proud to be himself?

Because of *him*.

Ah, yes. *Him*.

As Andrew pulled on his pajama bottoms and a baggy T-shirt, he tried for possibly the millionth time to figure out why *he* had so much power over him.

Teddy, otherwise known as Theodore Goldbloom — son of a business tycoon — with blond locks befitting his name and a killer smile that could stun a person at twenty paces. In high school, the boy had been gorgeous, head of the jock clan and made pretty decent grades as well.

The full package. The allusive triple threat. From a wealthy family, beautiful *and* smart.

Bastard.

Andrew was twenty-six and still ruled by the torment his sixteen-year-old self had lived through. That was the point. Andrew had survived that hell and had pulled himself up to where he was today.

But he didn't own this new, carefully created, better version of himself.

With people who didn't know him, he could play the part well enough. He could be the aloof computer genius. On the other hand, anyone who did know him turned him right back into a shaking mess who had run away.

After all these years, though, he'd finally realized one thing—you can't outrun the past.

Chapter Two

Andrew was almost sure he was certifiably insane for coming back without being dragged kicking and screaming. Standing in his apartment making the decision to return had seemed almost freeing, but now he had the urge to run as fast as he could in the other direction. However, he couldn't leave yet.

Something had been bugging him about part of the information he'd seen pass through Martin's server. Monitoring his boss wasn't illegal or the wisest thing he could be doing but every time he spoke to Martin, his instincts flared, telling him there was something not to be trusted about the man and that Andrew should be careful.

It seemed his paranoia was proving correct. Martin was up to his neck in trouble. His boss had been transferring information to outside CIA-sanctioned servers.

Andrew took his custom-built tablet out of his bag to browse through some of the files he knew Martin had looked at recently. It didn't take more than a few keystrokes to set up a secure Internet connection via his phone signal and encrypt his devices. That way, if anyone took an interest in what he was doing, the person would only see generic Internet browsing behavior. He called it the Window Shopper Program. Not even the other techs he'd befriended on various jobs had been able to recognize it as a program, let alone hack it.

Andrew was particularly proud of that.

The information he suspected Martin had sold had no common denominator other than it was high profile and it appeared to have been assigned to other supervisors in the agency, even though he knew it was a case Martin worked. On its own merits, there was no link to Martin but Andrew knew the man's code and there was definitely something off about the whole thing.

Everything consisted of coding in this day and age — all the digital stuff anyway. On the surface, the encryption within Martin's communications looked fine, but when Andrew delved deeper, he saw the recipients of a few messages were almost too clean, too polished.

The only person he knew with cypher this clean was himself. He'd spent years secretly cleaning up his code. With every camera that recorded a person, every time someone logged in to work or on his or her computer, even to communicate with someone through a device, a person always left a trail. That's how Andrew found people of interest for the CIA.

He studied the code, trying to figure out what exactly was wrong with it. The pattern relayed monetary transactions from Martin to unknown recipients. The unknown element angered Andrew.

He smacked the tablet screen, exiting the analysis program. He should have seen it earlier — the code had been altered. When it came to watching Martin, he should have been more vigilant.

This wasn't going to help anyone now. The agents and assets from the jobs that had been compromised were either lost or dead. Andrew should have noticed everything earlier. The only thing he could do now was figure out a way to stop Martin from doing this again.

Sighing in frustration, Andrew disabled the connection and swiped his tablet into 'off' mode, then shoved it back in his bag.

He looked out of the window and had to put a hand to his stomach to try to quell the urge to throw up over the nice old lady in front of him. There it was. A field, just a field. Anyone walking past it wouldn't give the place a second look. It was part of some old farmland that had overgrown.

To him it was the place where he'd lost everything. He'd lost people he'd thought were his friends. He'd lost his naïveté and belief that people were essentially good at heart. And he'd lost his best friend and first love.

Then just as quickly as the scene came into view, it disappeared as the bus turned the corner and headed to the center of town. The bus came out this way about once a week, and even then, only when the company called ahead that they had someone coming or going to or from the town.

Blackfields wasn't a small town, really. It was just quiet and the people in it tended to be security conscious when it came to their privacy.

Now that he thought about it, Andrew knew he could name at least a handful of people who pulled home about six figures a year. One or two even had secret bank accounts with a few million stashed away in foreign countries. Even as a teen he'd had a knack for computers, and the school curriculum had done nothing to challenge him.

Neither had the CIA firewalls, though, which is why he now worked for them.

Sort of.

A hard bump in the road shook Andrew out of his head and he realized the bus was pulling up to the outskirts of town. No vehicles entered the town without someone knowing about it and the local sheriff had never taken kindly to strangers, even the ones who were just passing through.

More than likely there were a few people who didn't want the general public to know where they lived when out of the limelight. Yeah. Blackfields was a weird town.

As soon as the bus stopped, Andrew got to his feet and wove down the aisle, dodging elbows and precariously stacked luggage. He got off the bus, waited for the driver to retrieve his suitcase from the hold then Andrew slipped him a decent tip before he was left standing alone, face-to-face with his past.

Andrew was here for a week and he was for damn sure going to face this once and for all. He was staying at a hotel not far from his parents' house and when he wasn't being dragged to the open invitation BBQ and formal dinner party he knew was planned, Andrew would deal with his nightmare.

By the end of this trip, Andrew was determined he would be able to put his feelings of fear and worthlessness behind him for good.

Then he was going to go home, get really drunk, and let some stud take him home and fuck him through the mattress.

He snorted at himself. "That's original."

It all sounded great but the idea a stud in a club would want him for a night of mindless, animalistic fucking was comedy gold. But spinning round drunk and no more fear sounded almost as good.

As *Meatloaf* sang, 'two out of three ain't bad'.

Gritting his teeth, Andrew slung his backpack over his shoulder and pulled the suitcase behind him as he took step after step. He could do this. He *would* do this. And fuck anyone who got in his way!

He managed to get to the hotel without being harassed but that ended at the front desk. He hoped he was wrong, but the woman manning the reception area looked very familiar. It was hard to tell what lay under the artificial tan. She looked an awful lot like Angela's friend, Millie.

Fingers crossed, he approached the desk.

The woman at reception pasted on a fake smile overladen with luminous pink lipstick. She blinked about six pairs of false eyelashes at him.

For a moment, Andrew was mesmerized by the creepy image of a Venus flytrap plant he'd had to look after in school. It had devoured a spider that looked just like her eyelashes.

Andrew shook off the heebie-jeebies and paid attention to what she was saying. At first, she was more interested in trying to sell herself than in giving him his key. "Call me if you need *anything*, Mr...?" The second he said his name, recognition hit Millie and the bubbly receptionist was gone as Millie the flying monkey came to the fore. She took one more look at him and almost threw his room key at him.

Andrew knew she would be texting the second he turned his back.

By the time he reached his floor, most likely everyone would know he was back in town. "Well, I might as well cancel that sky writing I ordered," he muttered as he turned and walked toward the elevators.

Sarcasm, it didn't work as well with just one person.

He kicked his suitcase over the bump as he entered the elevator and stabbed the floor number he wanted. He must have been insane to think he'd ever get closure by coming back here.

He got out and dragged his stuff to the door. The room he'd booked was the biggest they had without it being a suite. If he had to be in this damn town then he was going to have a good room that he could hide in.

Andrew put his suitcase in the corner and lay his bag with his laptop and computer equipment on the black wooden desk. There was also a black leather sofa that looked polished enough he could check his teeth in its shine.

Buzzing in his pocket reminded him he had to let Sara know he was here. He texted her.

Just got to hotel, room two-oh-three. Bring food?

She texted him back.

On way. Genie brought sustenance.

Sustenance? Someone was using the new thesaurus text app.

His second eldest sister Genie owned and was head chef of the most successful restaurant in town.

Even though he hadn't been there, he'd kept tabs on everything. In the first few months of it opening, rival business owners had tried to drown out the customer base with false reviews of horrible service and bad food.

He'd traced all of them back to two IP addresses and had sent a nasty virus their way, deleting any trace of the reviews. Just because he didn't want to come home didn't mean he didn't love his family.

He sent her another message.

Bring Genie too. Can catch up before doomsday.

She replied with a quick text.

Was anyway, Drew. XxX ;)

A sucky day of traveling and a rude receptionist aside, Andrew was looking forward to seeing his sisters. Sara and Genie, anyway. They used to hang out a lot when he lived here, even though they were older and had their own places.

He lost count of the times they'd patched up his scrapes and put ointment on his bruises after a run in with Angela's jock squad.

Every incident he'd had to beg them not to tell their parents. At the time, he'd thought he was doing it to save their feelings but now, looking back at it all, he realized he'd been protecting himself.

Back then he hadn't thought they'd believe him.

It was his biggest fear.

Knocking at the door yanked him out of the past. Glancing at the phone still in his hand, he saw fifteen minutes had passed. Shaking his head, Andrew turned and went to answer the door.

Sure enough, Genie and Sara stood on the other side and he'd barely turned the handle and flipped the automatic lock off when they barged in. Between the two of them, they took over his room in a way only big sisters could.

"Drew!" Genie hugged him.

Andrew found himself in a sister sandwich. He let them hold him and buried his face in Sara's long blonde hair. It was comforting and familiar and something he'd missed since their last visit.

"We missed you, Drew."

"I go by Andrew now," he corrected automatically.

He asked them to call him that every time, but they never did. The use of his full name was just another feather in the new identity hat.

"Pffft, don't try that with me, little bro. You'll always be Drew, my baby brother the computer genius," Genie cooed, still holding him tight from behind, resting her head on his back.

"Speaking of..." Sara leaned back and pinned him with a pointed look and an arched brow.

Well that was quicker than he'd expected.

"Are you finally going to spill the beans willingly or do we have to get rough?"

Genie and Sara broke the hug and Andrew realized he was outnumbered. And he wasn't going to be able to talk his way out of trouble.

"Uh..." He had nothing.

Genie came around to stand by Sara and they both took a step forward as he took one backward. With wicked grins, they advanced on him and he backed up until his legs hit the sofa.

"D-don—"

His sisters leaped at him. They all tumbled onto the sofa in a pile of awkward limbs and sharp elbows.

A few unfortunately placed knees had Andrew red-faced and tear-streaked as Genie and Sara sat on his back, smushing his face into the shiny leather.

"So are you going to talk, *Drew*, or do we have to break out the big guns?" Genie asked.

One of his sisters grabbed his foot while the other removed his shoes and socks.

They wouldn't. Would they?

Sara ran her fingertip down the sole of his foot and gave him his answer.

Andrew bucked and tried to throw his siblings off so he could get away. In the last few years, his sisters must have been working out, because they stuck fast to his back and never released their holds on his feet.

This was cruel and unusual punishment.

But effective. The CIA could learn something from them.

In under two minutes, Genie and Sara had him crying and begging to be let go.

"No! Get off me. For the love of God, please stop!" Out of breath, he ached all over from the unprovoked tickle attack as he crawled off the couch when they finally released him.

Andrew lay on the carpet as his nerves recovered from the assault. This was not how he saw his night going. He'd figured for some food, gossip and light-hearted teasing before collapsing into a food coma until morning.

Never in his life did he remember being so happy, sore and worried all at the same time. Andrew snorted. Okay, maybe he *could* think of a few occasions that description hit the mark.

Not one of those had involved women, though—and definitely not his sisters. An involuntary shudder zipped through him at the mere thought of girl parts.

"I give. I give." He panted, squeezing his eyes shut and trying to lift his arms to ward off another attack.

Though they'd released him, he had no doubt they'd jump on him with no warning if they thought he was being untruthful. His sisters could be paid well as interrogators for the CIA. Perhaps he should put in a good word for them.

A thump on either side of him on the floor startled him into opening his eyes. Sara sat on his left and Genie to his right. The carpet was comfy and Andrew did not intend to move yet.

Evidently, his sisters didn't mind lying on the floor, either, as they waited patiently. All three of his sisters, including the Evil One, had long blonde hair, straight and silky. They were also all blue-eyed, tall and athletic.

He was quite the anomaly. He was fairly short and thin with green eyes and curly chestnut hair that grew in ringlets if he let it get too long.

A poke to his side reminded him he was supposed to be talking. Taking a deep breath, he started at the beginning.

"When I went to college I wasn't in a good place mentally. And that is not something I will ever discuss with either of you, so don't ask me to," he started, meeting their gazes one at a time to make his point.

That was one thing about his life he never wanted his sisters to know.

They obviously saw his resignation since they didn't push. The identical pinches around their eyes told him they were going to worry about what he hadn't said anyway.

Tough. He wasn't going there.

"Anyway... I couldn't sleep, didn't eat much and didn't want to look after myself at all. I started playing around with computers. At first it was just the school mainframe, changing a few grades and classes here and there but it quickly got out of hand."

Genie gasped, and Andrew sensed the daggers Sara was glaring at him. Damn, he hadn't even gotten to the bad part yet.

Licking his lips, he forged on to the details he knew they were going to have a *real* problem with. "Then I got a little... Shall we say, overambitious? I may have hacked into the CIA cold case files. I also may have even solved a few of them by hacking into suspects' histories then making the file with the added information print out in one of the midlevel agent's offices."

Clenching his eyes shut, he waited for the explosion.

"You did *what*?"

Sara's shriek almost perforated his eardrum.

"How could you do something like that?"

Genie didn't have quite same shrillness but it still made him wince when it was directly in his ear. He opened his eyes.

Sara sat up and threw her hands in the air. Always the drama queen. It wasn't as though he'd told her about the time he'd accidentally found international diplomats' itineraries or the time he'd almost wiped out a professor's retirement fund, because the man had had an affair with his best friend and had broken her heart. She hadn't known he was married — or that he had three kids under five.

A sigh made him look back to Genie and he smirked when he saw her watching Sara with a similar expression of exasperation. She turned to him and tried to look stern. But Andrew could spot the tiny twitch at her lips.

"Sorry, sis. I wasn't in a good place." He shrugged.

"I'm not saying what you did was right and if anyone asks, I gave you a good ass-chewing. I do have to say I'm a little proud of you. The CIA! Awesome," Genie gushed with a grin. She pushed her bangs out of her eyes, making it stand up in tufts.

Surprised at her reaction, Andrew looked away and tried to ignore the way his cheeks burned. "Not as awesome as I'd thought. I got caught." He flinched as Sara screeched again.

"What!"

"Take a pill or something, Sara. Get a grip." Genie glared at their older sister. Speaking to him this time, Genie asked him a question. "What happened when they caught you?"

So he went on to explain how three agents had shown up at his dorm room one day after class and had basically given him an ultimatum—work for them or go to jail. And here he was so many years later, in deeper than he'd expected, and looking for a way out.

"You think your boss is dirty?"

"This isn't a cop show. People don't really say 'dirty' anymore."

"I beg to differ, Drew. Just the other day there was a man on the news and they had a caption underneath his picture saying 'this guy is a dirty cop'," Sara said smugly.

"Okay, fine. Whatever. Anyway, I know there's something wrong somewhere. There are too many discrepancies for it to be a coincidence but I have no idea who I can approach about it without getting my ass killed."

Either way, he was fucked. *Damned if you do and damned if you don't.*

On the one hand, he didn't think his conscience would allow him to continue to look the other way when things didn't add up on an assignment. However, he really didn't want to be locked up, tortured for information or killed.

"Killed?"

"It's the CIA," Andrew pointed out.

Silence filled the room.

"Shit," both sisters exclaimed at the same time.

"And now you see my problem," he said tiredly.

His sisters were quiet for a long while, leaning on him as if he were a cushion. It would have been relaxing if he wasn't dwelling on the trouble he was currently in. At least he wasn't thinking about Teddy.

Well, he *hadn't* been until now, anyway.

Genie sat up then sprang to her feet. She dragged him to stand too before racing over to his laptop bag and helping herself to its contents. She took out his equipment and, with surprising knowledge, set up his computer and the little device he'd created for secure, untraceable Internet usage.

"Uh, Genie?"

"Quiet," she shushed, waving her hand at him dismissively as she continued messing with his things.

It was as if he'd stepped into the Twilight Zone. Genie was so technophobic she could barely work a washing machine and now she was using his equipment as if she were the expert.

When the password screen came up, Genie turned and looked him up and down before typing something into the box. From where he was standing, he could see what she typed — S-P-O-C-K-N-C-C-1-7-0-1. The incorrect password sign flashed up.

After pushing her aside gently, he typed in his correct password, looked at her and waited.

There was no way he was going to comment on her knowing the password he'd used on his computer all the way through high school. He was a nerd and Spock was cool to him. Hot too in the new movies.

"Do your searching stuff and look for Agent Christopher Hammer," she ordered.

The look on her face told him he wasn't going to get anything more out of her until he obeyed.

At this point, Sara was looking at them both as if they'd each grown another head and had turned purple.

He brought up his search protocols and entered the name. There was nothing on the Net but he kept digging. Within a few minutes, he'd turned up quite a bit of information, not least of which was that the man was connected to a few corruption cases in the alphabet agencies.

Holy shit.

"How the hell do you know this man, Genie?"

"I dated him for a while last year before I figured out he was bi with a strong leaning toward your side of the fence. We chat when he's on assignment abroad, which is why I know how to set up your secure thingies. We're friends and I'm sort of his beard, I guess you'd say, when he needs to be seen with a girlfriend," Genie explained with a shrug as if what she'd done were an everyday occurrence.

Who knew, maybe for her it was. Andrew always figured beautiful people lived completely different lives to the rest of the ordinary ones. Hell, he'd be moving up in the world if he were one of the ordinary people.

Shaking his head, he ignored the comment about his 'secure thingies' and continued sifting through the information. The man seemed honorable, had served two short tours overseas before being recruited somewhere. That's when everything went a little blacked out. There was a lot of classified stuff in the file he'd found but a few hours under his software should clear that up if he needed to delve further.

From what Andrew could see, Agent Christopher Hammer was a decent man and good at his job. Apart from a speeding ticket from when he was a teen and a written warning for 'reckless behavior in pursuit of the enemy in combat' the man was clean. Squeaky even.

"Reckless behavior? What kind of man is he, Genie? You could be in danger! I knew you two were going to be trouble the second Mom popped you out." Sara sighed but it was an improvement from shrieking any day.

"Yeah, right. Your life would be more boring than drying paint without us, and you know it," Genie shot back with a mock glare.

Sara stood for a second, mouth in a comical O. She snorted. "Yeah, probably. So what do we do now?"

"We? A second ago you were squealing and looked like you needed a Valium and now you what? Want to take on the CIA?" Andrew couldn't help the skepticism leaking through into his words.

"Okay. Officially putting aside our family drama." Genie put her hands on his shoulders and made him face her. "I think maybe Chris can help you. He's dealt with corruption with other agencies before. He never told me specifics but a few comments here and there when we used to watch those crime shows makes me think he can help you. I wouldn't put you in danger, Drew," she said softly, placing a kiss on his head.

He didn't know what to think or what to do.

"Okay. Call your friend and see if he can come and meet me somewhere." He sighed, hoping he wasn't making a big mistake. Another thing was bugging him, though. "How did you know where everything was and how to use it when you set up my laptop and equipment?"

Genie's cheeks reddened and she dropped her gaze, apparently finding something interesting on the floor. "I don't know what the stuff is but Chris showed me how to use some of it before he went on his last tour so we could, um, talk."

"Oh, *talk*. Yeah, I know how to use the computer for that too." Sara chuckled.

Huh? Why would Genie be blushing *about talk — oh. Oh.*

"Ah! Brain pictures! Get them out!"

Slapping his forehead did nothing to dispel the disturbing images in his head but one look from his sisters made him rethink vocalizing his discomfort.

"Hey it's not like I'm giving you images of me having sex via the Internet, so give me a break. You're my sisters and therefore shall forever be virginal and chaste. Even if you have kids one day."

"Dreeeeew," his sisters said simultaneously.

They shook their heads at him but he saw the smiles they were trying to hide and he relaxed.

"Call your friend, Genie," he stated. "Then we can veg."

* * * *

Genie had called her friend and said he would be in town the day after tomorrow. They'd vegged for a few hours and watched some films. He'd been happy to pay for the films, since it was a Pay-Per-View channel but Sara had asked if he could do his mojo on it. Apparently, little Miss Hair Extensions at the front desk couldn't stop flirting with Steve.

Sara's long-time boyfriend was loyal, so there was no fear of him stepping out on his sister but the big man was also very polite and hated confrontation. Unless someone messed with Sara then the Hulk came out of the woodwork.

According to Genie, the woman was still Angela's best friend and routinely tried to seduce married men on their business trips. So it was for a good cause.

He'd rearranged the billing for his room to include complementary films and room service. He also made it look to anyone checking the reservation and booking system as though the woman had tried to do the same thing for every male guest there.

"Done," he told them, logging out of the system.

It should be enough to get Millie put on review, where management would have to keep a close eye on her. Somehow, he'd never imagined telling his sisters the truth about what he did would end in service requests. He kind of liked it.

It was probably the only thing about his visit that would go better than expected.

"Aw. Our little bro, the computer genius. If only you'd use your powers for good." Genie laughed before clearing her throat then did her impersonation of Spiderman's uncle. "With great power comes great responsibility."

"Urgh. When you two reproduce, I'm going to remind you of all the dumb shit you did when you were younger. Then tell your spawn all about those times you were chased off old man James' land for skinny dipping," he threatened.

"You do and I'll kill you, little brother." Sara narrowed her eyes with the threat.

Genie just kept laughing.

A tight, pained look crossed Sara's face before she hid it. "Speaking of kids... Steve and I are thinking of adopting. How would you feel about being an uncle?"

"Seriously?" Andrew wasn't sure what kind of role model he'd be but he loved the thought of being an uncle. But why would that make Sara look like she was seconds away from bursting into tears.

"We've been trying for a few years, but it doesn't look like being someone's biological mom is in the cards for me." Her voice broke and a single tear trickled down her cheekbone.

"Why didn't you say anything?" Genie immediately went to Sara and hugged her close as they both started crying.

"Sara?" Andrew edged closer, trying to get their attention. He put his arms around them and let them hug it out for a little longer before trying again. "Sara?"

Both sisters had stopped crying but didn't seem to be in a rush to let go of each other.

"I'll help you any way I can through the adoption processes but if you want to try IVF or any other fertility treatments to see if they could work for you, I'll help you with that too," he offered. No matter how much they nagged or teased him, he loved Sara and Genie. They were the two people in the world he would gladly do anything for.

Genie sat back, letting Sara go, and Andrew found himself with a lap full of big sisters.

"Umph!"

"Oh, Drew. You're so sweet. Any help you can give us with the adoption applications would be amazing. I barely understand some of the stuff. But fertility treatment is just too expensive. Steve doesn't earn much as a fireman and everything I earn at the store we have to use to pay off the house for the next few years." Sara buried her head in his shoulder.

The wetness of more tears penetrated his shirt.

She was so upset at the thought of not being able to get pregnant. He felt so guilty for not picking up on all the little clues. And why hadn't he seen they were struggling money-wise? He'd been so wrapped up in his own issues that he'd missed it.

"I'm so sorry I didn't see," he said, clinging to her tighter.

"You have nothing to be sorry for," Sara whispered, patting his cheek.

He knew she was just trying to make him feel better.

"Sara if you want to do IVF or anything like that, anything that might be able to give you what you want, then all you have to do is ask. I have enough money for anything and everything you could possibly try," Andrew tried to reassure her, rubbing her back and looking at Genie for help.

"But... How?"

Pointing to himself, he smiled. "Computer genius, remember? And apart from the possibly dirty boss, the CIA is a pretty good job. And I invested the small amount Gran left me online and that turned out well. Trust me. I have the money if you want it. I just wish you'd said something before."

He got another crying sister hugging him. It wasn't a sacrifice to offer his money. Sara and Steve needed it, and he had it to give.

Chapter Three

The next day, Andrew woke up with a headache. But the banging wasn't just inside his head. Someone was at his door.

Checking the clock, he saw it was only six in the morning. Damn, he'd forgotten everyone around here got up at the ass crack of dawn.

Andrew crawled out of bed and grabbed his jeans before dragging them on. "I'm coming!"

The knocking stopped as he made his way across the room.

Just as he got to the door and flipped the lock open, a yawn caught him. He opened the door. Strong arms came around him like restraints and trapped him against a wall of a hard chest.

He struggled but couldn't see who it was and he couldn't get free. Just as he was about to try yelling for help, he was released.

He tried to stay on his feet but his innate clumsiness took over and he stumbled, feet twisting until he landed hard on his backside.

"No!" Andrew shouted and tried to scramble backward while lifting his arms to ward off any blows. Flashbacks of all the times he'd been caught alone by the jock squad came back to haunt him.

His chest tightened with fear and he couldn't get enough air. Oh God, it was happening again. They'd come for him. Andrew tried harder to get away and swung his arms.

"It's okay. I'm sorry. It's just me. I won't hurt you, Drew."

Instantly relieved, Andrew climbed to his knees. It was just Steve, Sara's boyfriend. The firefighter. Not someone who was there to hurt him.

"Are you all right, Drew?" Steve crouched next to him, hands out as if to appear unthreatening. The man was six-foot-seven and had shoulders wider than two of Andrew.

Gradually, his breathing returned to normal and he let Steve help him stand. One positive was that he was definitely awake now. There was nothing like heart-stopping fear to get him up and moving in the morning.

"I'm really sorry, Drew. I swear I didn't mean to scare you," Steve said, sounding racked with guilt.

As big as Steve was, he was the epitome of the gentle giant. The man was perfect for Sara with his laid-back attitude and easy-going nature. It was hard to stay mad at him.

"It's okay. I'm just jumpy," he replied quietly and shrugged.

Shuffling his feet, he tried not to stare as Steve took his coat off and hung it up on the rack. Steve was buff and the T-shirt did nothing to hide it. Sara often teased him about getting distracted with Steve's muscles.

Suddenly he was keenly aware that he was only wearing jeans and that his pale, bony chest was on display. He looked down at himself then back at Steve. Damn.

Turning, he stalked over to his bag and dug out a shirt. He pulled it over his head without looking at it. A laugh from beside him made him jump and he glanced up to see Steve grinning at his T-shirt.

No. It couldn't be.

Sure enough there was a picture of a buff, half-naked man in a yellow helmet, sliding down a metal pole with the phrase 'want to see my pole?' written underneath in glitter.

"Kill me now."

Steve got out his phone and snapped a photo, no doubt to send to Sara. Damn it, this was getting to be a bad day already and he hadn't been up ten minutes.

"Come on, Drew. You knew she was going to get you to wear it sooner or later. She told me she sneaked it in your bag yesterday. This photo will be printed and framed within the hour," Steve joked, waving the phone.

It would be funny if it weren't true. This would be on the front of birthday and holiday cards for him for his foreseeable future. Great.

"What can I do for you, Steve?" He liked the man but he was tired, annoyed and wanted a long, hot shower before he ventured out to visit his parents.

Steve came toward him slowly and pulled him into a hug. One big hand came up to cup his head and press it closer to Steve's chest and the other Andrew could feel gripping the back of his T-shirt in a tight fist.

He still wasn't keen on people touching him but Steve was family.

"I wanted to thank you. Thank you. Thank you for giving her a chance to have a child," Steve whispered over and over in his ear.

"Hopefully the specialist I found last night will be able to help her," Andrew answered, trying and failing to pull out of the hug. "Let me go, Hulk, or Sara will have my ass for copping a feel." He laughed.

He only had so much control. And Steve was hot. Pressed against Steve like this was going to cause an embarrassing reaction for both of them.

Steve smiled at his attempt at humor but stepped back.

"She would love any child we adopted like her own but she longs to feel what it's like to be pregnant."

They'd make great parents and he was glad he could help—whether the fertility worked or whether they went the adoption route.

"Does this mean you're finally going to marry my sister?" He was joking but he'd wondered over the years why they hadn't tied the knot.

"Yes. We've been waiting to drag you home so we could do it right. She's calling in reinforcements as we speak, so don't be surprised if you get roped into doing something. Which brings me to the other reason for me coming here."

"At the ass crack of dawn," he pointed out.

Steve didn't take the dig to heart. He just gave him a stunning smile. "City boy. My fellow firefighters will be there as my family since I have none. But will you be my best man?"

The reminder that Steve was the last of his kin made Andrew feel a little guilty that he hadn't made the effort to come home more for the family he loved.

Then the rest of what Steve said sank in. Best man? What, him?

"I... I... I..." He literally couldn't get any words out.

Luckily, Steve was used to him and his selective mutism and stuttering. "Just say yes, Drew."

"Yes," he croaked, nodding obediently.

"Good. Now I need to get to the station. Stop by after you've seen your parents and I'll show you my pole." With a wink, Steve grabbed his coat and left before Andrew had time to process the last bit.

After tugging the T-shirt off, Andrew balled it up and threw it on the bed. He was never going to hear the end of this. Resigned to his fate, he headed to the bathroom for a long shower.

* * * *

Andrew stood on his parents' walk and desperately tried to think of a reason not to knock on the door. Taking the half dozen steps one at a time, he held out hope he might slip and have to be taken to hospital.

No one could say that wasn't a credible excuse.

The last step came and went and he was still safe and sound. Damn. There went that plan. He bent to pick up the newspaper from the welcome mat.

Before he straightened, the door opened and he was face-to-face with his father's slippers.

"Drew? Son, is that you?"

Standing, he handed the paper over to his father and tried to remember to breathe normally. Being back was harder than he thought it would be.

His father looked him up and down.

Andrew's skin crawled as familiar feelings of inadequacy and lacking resurfaced. "Hi Dad," he muttered.

His father just turned and walked inside.

"You better come in," his dad said.

Now there was a warm welcome.

No place like home, indeed. He stamped on the words printed on the welcome mat and entered the house.

"Susan? Drew's home." In typical dad fashion, the old man walked into the dining room and sat, opening the newspaper to hide behind it. Some things never changed.

It was hard to believe this was the man who had taught him how to use his first computer and who'd played soccer with him in the park.

"Oh! Drew, you're home," his mother cried, running out of the kitchen and throwing her arms around his neck as if he were back from war or something.

"Hi, Mom." Andrew hugged awkwardly and tried to bite back the urge to correct her. He really hated when people called him Drew. He wasn't that kid anymore.

His mother stood a good few inches shorter than him and still wore her blonde hair in a long braid that trailed over her shoulder. Pulling out of the hug, he looked at her. There were a few more wrinkles and crowfeet at the corner of her eyes but she was still beautiful. Genie and Sara had her warmth and beauty while Angela only had their mother's hair.

His mother brushed his bangs back with her fingers and looked at him. There was a good bit of sadness in that look and, if he had to put a name to the other emotion, he would say it was shame.

Why would his mother be ashamed when she looked at him? He didn't think it was because he was gay. Both of his parents hadn't been thrilled when he'd told them but they hadn't been ashamed of him either.

"I'm so glad you've finally come home, son," his mother whispered, her eyes shining wetly.

"Let him be, Susan," his dad spoke up from behind his paper.

Her face changed from beautiful to angry in a flash, stunning Andrew with the sheer intensity he saw there.

Before Andrew could even try to come up with a topic change, his mother spun around, stomped over to his father and ripped the paper from his hands. "You listen to me, you stubborn old fool. We spoke about this and we are going to fix this damn family with or without you. So pick a side, Norman," she shouted, pointing a delicate finger.

His father blustered and turned a vivid shade of red but said nothing back.

"Uh, what's going on?"

Never in his life had he witnessed something that left him in such complete and utter shock. Andrew couldn't ever remember his mother raising her voice, let alone talking to his father like that.

There was silence as his parents had a stare off, each trying to make the other back down.

After a minute, his father sighed and rubbed a hand over his face. "All right, Susan. All right."

Both his parents turned to Andrew. He noticed the shadows of stress around his father's eyes, the dark bags under them and the way his clothes hung on him as though they were two sizes too big.

He should have been here. He should have helped. The thought shocked him enough that he almost didn't hear when his father started talking.

"I've been ill for a while but we made the decision not to let you kids know until it was time."

His father's voice was strong but the shake in it had Andrew rushing to his dad's side and grasping his hand.

No matter how much Andrew hated home, he still loved his parents.

"Are you okay, Dad?"

His father looked surprised then gripped his hand and smiled a little. "The doctors say that the cancer is all but gone and the chemo worked well. I have to have check-ups every month for a year but I'm fine."

"You are not fine, Norman. You have to gain at least twenty pounds before I'll agree that you are better," his mother interrupted. She went to sit on the other side of her husband and took his other hand.

"Yes, dear." This time there wasn't any anger in his father's tone, just love.

Andrew's parents hugged and shared a brief kiss before turning back to him.

His father studied him for a second or two then spoke calmly. "We didn't want to tell anyone until we knew for certain which way things were going to go."

"Which way… So you could have died and not told any of your children?" Andrew was at a loss at how to deal with this.

After all the years he'd spent running away from his family and this place, never once had the thought crossed his mind that one day no one would be here when he came back. He'd assumed his parents would always be here.

"No, son. When the doctor gave me an answer as to where I stood with the cancer, we were going to tell you kids together. We just found out yesterday that the chemo worked. Your sisters don't know yet. They should be here any minute now," his father rushed to explain.

The reassurance that his parents were going to tell them and that his father's cancer was under control quickly disappeared with the announcement that his sisters were about to arrive.

"All of them?" Andrew asked.

"Yes, why?" His mom offered him a puzzled look.

"So A-A-Angela is c-c-coming here. N-n-n-ow?"

His heart started racing and his skin grew clammy. He didn't want to see Angela. This was his worst nightmare. What the hell had made him think he could do this, face her? Andrew needed to get out of there — now.

"Yes. Drew, what's wrong? You look like you're having a panic attack. You're worrying me." His mother was suddenly at his side, brushing his hair back. She put her hand on his forehead as she used to do when he was little to check his temperature.

The doorbell rang and Andrew really started to panic. He stood, knocking his chair over. His mother gasped.

Ignoring the questions of what the hell was wrong with him, he tried to stumble toward the kitchen. The back door. He needed to get to the back door so he could escape.

"I need t-t-to leave," he stuttered, clawing at the neck of his T-shirt to ease the choking tightness in his throat.

"No, you are staying right there, Drew. We need to figure this out now. This has been going on long enough."

Genie's calm voice let him know the escape wasn't going to happen. It was too late.

Andrew had no control over his body as he let Genie hold him and spun around in slow motion. He came face-to-face with the monster of his nightmares—Angela.

First off, Angela was stunning. But the longer a person spent in her company the more her inner ugliness crept to the surface, making the features that were once smooth and glowing, sharp and cruel.

"Hello, *little* brother."

Her voice burned him like acid as he flinched away from her.

"Drew?"

He didn't look back as his father called him.

"Don't tell me you're still hung up on that little prank?" Angela said. "Oh, my God, you are! How pathetic." Her cackle echoed in the silent room.

Andrew shook uncontrollably as his stomach turned over wildly. Unable to stop himself, he ran out of the room.

He couldn't get to the door since Angela blocked the way but he managed to make a beeline for the bathroom. Not a moment too soon, he collapsed to his knees in front of the toilet and lifted the lid before he became violently ill.

"It's okay, baby. Everything will be okay," Genie soothed him little by little, as she rubbed his back.

After a few minutes, the attack on his insides had ended and he pulled the lever, flushing and closing the lid. With Genie's help, he dragged himself to the sink and washed his face.

A toothbrush with toothpaste already on it appeared in front of his face. When he had finished, a glass of mouthwash was set in front of him.

"Thank you," he croaked, his throat raw and abused.

Genie nodded.

He saw shiny, wet streaks trailing down her face.

"She really is evil, isn't she?" Genie asked.

Not that Andrew was disagreeing but he was curious as to what had brought about this sudden revelation. He knew his other sister had a soul as dark as coal, but Genie always tended to see the best in people.

"Sara told me about Mr Robinson. He's decided to press charges. And she's going to tell Mom that she's going to the police tomorrow," Genie confessed.

"Holy shit."

But he had a mouth full of mouthwash so it came out as a weird gargle and he accidently swallowed the stuff. The liquid burned sickly minty all the way down his throat.

"Yeah, that pretty much sums it up. I don't know what that bitch did to upset you so badly but I swear to God if I see her in town I'll rip her to pieces," Genie promised.

She held his hand as they walked back to the living room where he knew everyone was most likely waiting for them — or waiting for more drama.

When they did enter the room, no one was there. Genie shrugged when he looked at her. He opened his mouth to ask the obvious question, but a crash and yelling came from the kitchen.

Rushing to the doorway, Andrew paused at the scene in front of him. His mother stood by the kitchen door next to Angela, who was red-faced and holding her nose. Their father held Sara's bleeding hand under the tap.

Chapter Four

Andrew studied the scene but Genie beat him to the question.

"What the heck is going on?" she asked.

Andrew drew up short as they entered the kitchen. How long had they been gone? Clearly he'd missed the pilot episode of this little drama.

Andrew looked from Sara, to his father, to Angela and back again. Talk about a watched pot never boils. Apparently the expression should be that if he stepped outside to throw up for a minute, the pot exploded.

"She fucking hit me!" Angela shrieked.

The words came out a garbled mess but Andrew understood the gist of the message when his mother pulled Angela's hands away from her face and blood started running down, staining Angela's white lace shirt.

He glanced from his father to his mother.

Genie took a step toward Angela and their mom. Andrew knew she really couldn't help it.

Peacemaking was in Genie's nature as the middle child.

"Don't you dare go to that bitch." Sara struggled to get her hand out of their father's grip but he held fast. She settled for just pointing as she shouted.

"Sara! Don't talk to your sister like that," their mother scolded, sending a hard look at her. "Genie, come help me."

Angela's nose still poured blood. Andrew sensed that Genie wanted to go and help, so he wasn't surprised when Genie moved closer. It did shock him, however, when she just picked up a dishcloth and merely handed it to their mom, not aiding in any other way.

"I'll talk to her any way I choose. You don't know half the shit she's done. And how could you let her get away with upsetting Drew that much? Do you actually realize what's gone on? Why he left in the first place? I don't. But I know damn well it has her brand of evil stamped all over it."

Everyone turned to look at him. He stood there like a deer caught in headlights. He really should have stayed in the bathroom.

"What's she talking about, Drew?" his father asked.

His dad's no-nonsense tone reminded him he needed to come up with some sort of response. "Nothing," Andrew stated. "I don't want to talk about it. Sara, now isn't the time." It really wasn't. And if he had his way, it never would be.

"You need to tell them," Sara insisted. "But that's not all the nasty little viper has done. You know your good friends, the Robinsons? Well, Mom, you're helping the slut who broke up their marriage."

This time Sara did slip out of their dad's hold and took a few steps closer to Angela before Andrew grabbed her around the waist and dragged her back to the sink. He pushed her bleeding knuckles under the tap again. Calming Sara once she was worked up was like trying to put out a forest fire with a tea towel.

"What the hell are you talking about?" their mother questioned. "What does a disagreement between Angela and Drew have to do with our friends?"

Angela's crying paused before renewing. Andrew guessed the Evil One was paying closer attention to what they were saying now. It probably wasn't in her master plan for everything to come out. Regardless, he wasn't going to hold his breath that the truth would mean anything to her. Hell and snowballs came to mind.

"A disagreement?" He couldn't stop the incredulous tone as he repeated his mom's words. How could he ever have thought he was wrong about them? It was going to be the same old routine. He shook his head and turned back to Sara. "Are you sure you want to do this *now*? This was supposed to be a happy talk." As far as he knew, Sara was going to announce her official engagement to Steve and that they were planning to explore adoption possibilities.

Sara flinched but she didn't back down. He tried glaring at her. Still nothing.

His mom was still fussing over Angela as his sister screeched that her nose better not be broken. From what Andrew could see, it wasn't just broken, it was also a little wonky.

Note to self, buy Sara a basket of mini muffins.

No doubt, Angela would get some plastic surgery to correct the superficial imperfection. Having an imperfect nose would be bad for her stellar reputation, he was sure.

"Sara, answer the question—and you, young lady," their mother firmly told Angela, "stay right here."

Angela tried to sneak away, but their mother kept a firm grip on Angela's arm.

"Angela drugged Mr Robinson," Sara explained, "slept with him then the plan was to blackmail him. But the man had a conscience and left the morning after, just packed up and left, because he was so ashamed of what he'd done."

"I don't understand," their mother stated.

Angela took advantage of her mom's distraction and stepped away, ripping the bloody cloth from her face. "God, he was so pathetic, crying about his fucking wife. He should have just gone along with it and paid me like I told him to."

"Angela, tell me you didn't," their mom begged.

Andrew knew it was a futile attempt. Angela only recognized one emotion as far as he could tell—greed. He knew for damn sure she only cared about herself.

Sara wasn't finished with Angela yet. Andrew guessed what she was going to say before she opened her mouth. A little part of him wanted her to lay it all out in the open so he could see how far his parents were willing to forgive or ignore.

"And guess what? Drew found Mr Robinson, and I have your bragging session with one of your flying monkeys recorded—with several copies. You won't get away with it this time." Sara trembled from head to toe by the end of her rant.

Andrew thought she was awesome. Sara's hair lay all over the place and her cheeks shone pink. There and then, he decided she was his new hero.

"You! You fucking ruin everything. I should have killed you when you were a baby," Angela screamed, throwing her venom at him this time.

It wasn't anything new from the Evil One but he was surprised she'd let her veneer slip when there were other people around.

This time Genie made a run for Angela, and Andrew wasn't close enough to stop her. Luckily, their dad stepped in front of Genie, who had to either stop or slam into him. She didn't look happy about the choice.

Their mother gasped and stepped back as the blood drained from her face.

Cheeks red with anger, Andrew's father pointed at the door. "Get out of my house, Angela! You're not welcome here anymore."

"Oh, like I care. I was hoping you'd die so I could at least get some money out of you, you stupid old fool," Angela spat, giving their dad a cold look.

Her outburst surprised Andrew. There was more than one screw loose in that mad bag of cats. She'd finally done it. Andrew looked around at his family and realized they finally saw his sister for who she really was.

His dad stepped back then tipped his head up, narrowing his eyes dangerously. Andrew had never seen him so mad before.

"Get out, or so help me God, I will let your sisters beat the hell out of you with my blessing."

Genie maneuvered around him. Her expression must have shown Angela how serious they all were. The Evil One smacked at her mother's hands and stormed out of the kitchen, slamming the door so hard a crack zigzagged in the window.

Hurricane Angela had left the building.

Broken window. Broken nose. Andrew really hoped nothing else was going to break. But these things tended to happen in threes.

"That child. I cannot even begin to put in to words how awful that child is," their mother choked out, holding a hand up to her face and erupting into shuddering sobs.

Ah, broken heart it is. And that completed the rule of three.

Genie ran over to her and sent Andrew and Sara a pleading look that had them both following close behind. He wasn't feeling particularly touchy-feely right now. Neither was he cruel enough to hurt his parents further by not trying to offer some comfort.

"It's okay, Mom," Genie said.

"It is *not* okay. My child is a horrible person," their mother cried as she pulled Andrew closer and wrapped her arms around him.

Her tears soaked the shoulder of his T-shirt but he wasn't thinking of ways to extract himself from the hold. It was sort of nice. Minus the crying, of course. The last time he'd had a mom hug like this, where he couldn't take a full breath, was when he'd graduated.

"Only one of us is. The rest of us are pretty all right," he joked, trying to lighten the mood.

It seemed to work when his mom calmed down and his dad snorted.

"You said it was time to pick a side, Susan. We chose the right one. Now we have to try and move on from here as a family," their father stated.

It was a wise thing to say but it made Andrew uncomfortable thinking about whatever the future might bring. Angela wasn't the type to lose or to let go of a grudge.

"Well, you can't say we don't know how to have a family reunion. *Jerry Springer Show* here we come," Andrew said.

"Drew," Sara and Genie exclaimed simultaneously.

Even his mother cracked a smile. "I think we'll be all right without a TV show." She pulled away from them and wound her arm through her husband's. "Despite how horrible all that was, this is the best I've seen you in a while, Norman. You wouldn't know you've been recovering from anything."

"I think I needed a good bit of drama to wake me up." He looked in Andrew's direction.

"We've noticed Dad was ill and we heard the announcement through the open window in the other room." Sara glared at both parents before kissing her father on the cheek. "I wish you'd told us sooner but I'm glad you're going to be okay, Daddy."

"Thank you, honey. And the first thing I'm going to do now that I have the 'all clear' is to re-teach you how to throw a decent punch, girl. I taught you better than that." Their dad shook his head in disgust.

Sara looked affronted but hissed when their father pressed an antiseptic wipe Genie had passed him against the torn skin of her knuckles.

Grinning, Andrew teased, "By the way, did anyone manage to catch the alleged nose breaking on camera so Genie and I can see what we missed? And why are your knuckles bleeding, anyway? Did she bite you or something?" He really couldn't help himself.

No one was as surprised as he was when their father let Sara go and patted her on the back proudly.

"Sara smacked that vicious little viper in the mouth but good. It wasn't until Angela shrieked that I realized I've been waiting for someone to do that for ten damn years."

"Norman!" His wife stepped back and placed her hands on her hips.

Andrew immediately put his guard up, thinking this was where the excuses would start. When he was growing up, every time he and Angela got into trouble his mother managed to explain away anything that had put Angela in a bad light.

"Be honest, Susan." His father stood up straight. "Neither of us wanted to believe Angela was like she is, and maybe if we hadn't stuck our heads in the sand Drew wouldn't have felt he couldn't come home and our friends would still have a marriage."

Andrew sensed his dad's gaze on him again. This time he met his father's eyes.

Just like that, his mom deflated and slumped as if the weight of the world had settled on her shoulders. "I know. I know," she whispered, wiping a stray tear off her cheek with the back of her hand.

Andrew hated seeing his mother cry but the devil on his shoulder took the tiniest bit of pleasure in the fact that Angela wasn't the golden girl anymore and that at least some of her crimes were now in the light.

* * * *

They'd all calmed down and gone to wash up before convening in the living room. Andrew had brushed his teeth again too. His mother was sitting on the brown, overstuffed sofa they'd had since he was little, and he, Genie and Sara were sitting on the double-seater recliner.

Andrew hid behind his cup of coffee when their father sat forward and cleared his throat as though he was about to say something important, something he wasn't entirely comfortable with.

"I think we need to get a few things out in the open."

Andrew glanced at Sara and Genie, expecting them to answer but they were both looking at him. Great. He'd obviously been nominated as spokesperson.

"What do you have in mind?"

Their father looked at their mom but she just nodded encouragingly and patted his knee. "I know we've done wrong by you," he said, "and I honestly don't have a reason why we didn't see what was going on or how alone you must have felt, Drew."

Andrew almost dropped his cup in shock.

Genie took the mug with a smirk and put it with hers on the coffee table.

His dad didn't look sick or weak. The argument with Angela seemed to have released a lot of tension in all of them—except for him anyway. Andrew's heart seemed a little hollow and bruised.

"I did feel alone," he admitted.

Sara and Genie leaned against him and he remembered that he wasn't that same little kid now. He was an adult and he was smart enough to know he wasn't alone. His sisters had stuck up for him, defended him and one may have even chipped Angela's perfect teeth, if he was lucky.

"I better not have hurt my hand for nothing. I forgive you for not coming to me before but if you run again, I'll... Do something you won't like," Sara finished with a yawn.

"Yup," Genie added. "We'll steal all the L keys off your computers."

Andrew couldn't help but smile at that. He didn't bother telling them he had a bag of spare keys in his apartment in case such a letter theft incident occurred. "Consider me warned."

There was a beat of heavy silence before their mom asked, "Are you really going to the police about what you have on Angela?"

Sara tensed. "I have an appointment tomorrow at the police station with Mr Robinson's lawyer."

"Good."

He wasn't the only one whose jaw dropped at their mother's response.

Andrew thought he'd hidden his reaction well by reaching up to adjust his glasses but his father saw it and frowned.

"You think we would have disagreed?" his dad questioned.

Genie answered before Andrew could and it was probably for the best. He wasn't in the most charitable mood right now.

"Well," Genie said, "in the past you haven't exactly been pro punishment for Angela."

Both their parents sighed before sharing a look. Andrew could almost see something passing between them.

"This isn't an excuse for our behavior but it might help you understand our side of things a little better. When I was pregnant with Angela, I had a dizzy spell at the top of the stairs and fell down them. We almost lost her and I spent two months on bed rest to prevent miscarrying."

Only a monster could have listened to the pain in his mother's voice and not felt something. The sight of his father wiping a tear off his mom's cheek and kissing her lightly almost broke Andrew's heart. He had no idea how scary that experience must've been for them.

"We aren't perfect by any stretch but we thought until recently we had been okay parents." His mom's breath hitched. "But when your father started to get sick we did a lot of revaluating. I'm so sorry, Drew."

"I still won't tell you what happened. It's not fair to expect me to after nine years of nothing but holiday small talk," he defended cautiously. Andrew didn't want to upset whatever this new equilibrium was, but he wasn't ready to ignore the voice in his head telling him not to trust them yet either. If they had been as protective of him as they had been of Angela then he wouldn't have had to run away in the first place.

His mother teared up again but she nodded. "I know. It will take time but I really hope you'll give us a chance to show you how proud we are of you."

"Proud?" The word was alien coming out of his mouth.

His father grabbed his attention again by standing and coming over to him. Andrew was too shocked to move. And even if he weren't, his sisters were weighing him down in case he ran. It was as if he'd entered the Twilight Zone a second time.

"We've always been proud of you, Drew," his father told him. "The early admission you got to college, the scholarships, your apartment, your job, this life you have in the city — *you* did that — and all on your own."

The acknowledgment made him blush and he reached up to fiddle with his glasses before he could deny the urge. A lot of his old habits were back.

"Oh. Th-th-th-thank you." He *had* done all that on his own. He'd never imagined his father ever telling him he was proud of what he'd done.

It seemed like everyone was waiting for him to say something but nothing would make sense in his head.

"With all that, it doesn't even matter that you're gay." His father smile like he'd said something good.

Even? Why did his dad have to say that, like being gay was something that had to be balanced out?

"Dad," Genie chastised.

"Not that there's anything wrong with being gay," his mother rushed to add, looking embarrassed.

It was too late. The damage had been done and the warm fuzzy feeling he'd had vanished, stamped out like a cigarette butt.

"Thank you." Andrew snatched his hand down from his glasses and sat up straighter as he retreated into the distant coldness he used as a mask in the city. From the look on his dad's face, Andrew knew the older man didn't know what he'd done wrong. Usually Andrew wasn't so touchy about the gay issue but he'd never officially come out to his parents. He'd never had to with the way he crushed hard on Spike in *Buffy the Vampire Slayer*. But in the face of saying everything he'd accomplished, it seemed like it was a bad mark. Andrew couldn't even say it was totally his dad's fault. The man was trying. Andrew could see that even as he withdrew. Perhaps the problem lay within himself.

Genie let him push her off his lap, but Andrew couldn't get up because she grabbed his hands and squeezed tightly.

She looked at him. "Let's change the subject, shall we?"

"Yes!" Sara said. "Steve and I are getting married. This weekend."

"Oh, that's wonderful!" Their mom jumped up and hugged Sara, patting Andrew on the cheek as well.

"I was wondering if we could hijack your birthday, Dad?"

"Of course. You know I hate birthday parties anyway."

"You do not." His mother gasped and spun around to pin his dad with a glare.

"I do when I have to pay for them and clean up after them," their dad mumbled.

Andrew had to laugh at that.

"So we have a guest list done, venue done, food covered by yours truly and decorations. That just leaves dresses, suits, photographer, cake, the good-luck list, rings, the officiate—you can get it legalized later if you have to—and flowers, music, favors and a million other things I'm sure I'll remember later," Genie rattled off the list.

Andrew's mouth dropped open. He couldn't believe the length of the to-do list. That was a hell of a lot to do in three days.

Clearly he wasn't the only one feeling a little nauseated.

"I was thinking of just a simple wedding," Sara said wide-eyed, looking a little panicked.

Their mother waved off Sara's words and started writing a list on the notepad she'd snatched up from the coffee table. There couldn't be that much stuff to organize, surely? All that mattered was the person you were getting married to, right? From the ever-growing list his mother was furiously scribbling, Andrew guessed not. This was a very bad idea.

"Well the most important thing is the dress. Steve can wear his dress uniform. Your bridesmaids will have to get dresses. And you need yours right away if you want to get it fitted before the day," their mom joined in the wedding mania with Genie.

His only ally was Sara and he could see her resolve crumbling away bit by bit as she succumbed to the temptations of handmade bunting for the decoration and little keepsake photo frames as favors.

He felt like shouting 'no, don't go to the dark side!' but he could already see the reasonable side of her disappearing and the bridezilla within bursting free. Andrew should have run when he had the chance.

"Can't you just wear something you already have or get a dress in town? I passed a couple of ball gown stores on my way into town. They'll probably have a white one." He'd thought his suggestion was useful but the death glares he was receiving from all three women told him otherwise. Yep. The mother ship was calling them home.

"Anyway. If you order the dress online it can be shipped here over night then you can get it fitted tomorrow." Genie was practically clapping like an overexcited child. "I can dust off my lace icing piping skills tonight at home and Mom can make the cake."

His mother ran out of the room then bustled back in carrying a laptop. It was a year or two old but it was a decent machine. Good speed, memory and was hard wearing for a laptop. Color him impressed too.

Their mother turned it on and quickly brought up an online wedding dress site and his sisters started crossing off dresses and styles as if they were a firing squad. One brilliant white dress hugged on the model's figure and flared out at the bottom. The vintage-style lace flowed down the sides, back and bodice with a simple sparkly veil. Sara would look stunning in that one. And it was hell of lot nicer than the stupid poofy things that looked like mutant marshmallows consuming the bride. However, he had a feeling if he pointed it out he'd be dragged into the madness.

The pictures were tiny on the site so he couldn't really see any of the detailing. Clicking on each individual dress page would take ages, so he took the laptop off the table and quickly typed in an algorithm that would display the dresses on the site on full screen until someone pressed enter then the next dress would display. It didn't take much to make sure the gown he'd spotted would come up onscreen multiple times.

When he was finished, Andrew wished he hadn't interfered. Now the women sat on him as they all pointed to the little details that they liked or hated. Could ears bleed from too much talk of tulle and whatever the hell underskirts were? And he didn't know what a boat neck was, either, but it sounded painful.

It was a bad thing to do but he couldn't stop himself. Andrew picked the tackiest dress that had come up so far and pointed at it. "What about that one? That's nice."

They all looked at it then turned to him.

Sara evidently was nominated to speak as the only woman not laughing at his choice. "Drew, I love you but you have no taste at all. Go do something useful and tell my husband-to-be that we'll be having a council of war meeting to discuss wedding plans today."

Their mom popped up from whispering behind the laptop lid and caught his attention. "Oh, and tell him we'll have a celebratory meal tonight, will you?"

"Oh, really? Bummer," he said as sincerely as he could manage.

From the way his dad's eyes narrowed, he guessed he hadn't pulled it off as well as he thought.

"Yes," Andrew replied, "I'll go tell Steve what you said right now."

He hightailed it out of the living room before his sister's brain started working again and she or Genie realized they'd been played. He heard steps behind him as he got to the door and turned around expecting to see one of his sisters. "You caught m — oh."

It was his dad.

"Can I talk to you for a minute, Drew?"

"Sure."

"I think you may have taken what I said earlier the wrong way. I don't think there's anything wrong with being gay or you being gay. I only meant..." His father brushed a hand over his face and rested his fingers where there used to be a short beard before he'd gotten sick. "I don't know what I meant. Dammit, I can't think of a way to say what I'm thinking. My words get muddled. The doctor said that would get better with time." He angrily smacked the wall.

Andrew flinched.

His father grimaced. "It's part of this new chemo treatment that temporarily affects my speech. The words are all in my head but sometimes I end up picking the wrong one."

"Oh." Andrew didn't know what else to say.

"I haven't been the father I ought. I should have been there for you to talk to but I was lost when your mother and I realized you didn't have any interest in girls and I didn't know how to talk with you. Son, I swear I didn't even know how much I was letting slip through the cracks with you until I thought I might die. My father wasn't a good man and I have my own anger toward him that I couldn't let go of until recently. It made me bitter and I don't want that for you. You haven't heard the words from me since you were too little to remember but I do love you, Drew. You're my boy." His father's eyes shone brightly by the end of the speech.

Andrew blinked as he tried to take in all that information. Everyone in the family knew there had been a lot of tension between their dad and Gramps but the old man had died years ago. It hadn't even occurred to him that his dad might have emotional issues too. It was strange seeing his father as a person instead of just his dad.

"It means a lot for you to say that but you know it's not going to make everything go away, right?"

His father nodded and they stood there for a short while in silence.

"I wanted to ask you whether sometime you might feel comfortable talking to me about whatever Angela did to you? And about your life—everything I missed?"

Bile rose up in Andrew's throat at the thought of telling his dad everything. It was a long list. "Maybe. Someday. But not right now," he hedged, answering as honestly as he could.

"I guess that's all I can ask for. I'll see you later for supper, then?" His father's expression suddenly changed and a big smile replaced the frown. "Your mother has been waiting years to work wedding plans for one of you kids. If you ditch and leave me with the mother of the bride craziness living inside your mother, I will personally come and drag you back here. Deal?"

"Uh, sure thing." Andrew smiled back then let out a laugh. The joking manner was odd but nice. He'd say anything right now to get out of the house and away from the wedding chaos that would undoubtedly ensue.

With the matter agreed upon, his father turned and started walking back to the living room. There was a relaxed line to his dad's shoulders that Andrew didn't remember seeing before. Things were by no means calm or all forgiven between them but it gave him hope.

"Hey, Dad? Thanks!" Andrew slipped out of the door and shut it behind him before his dad could even turn around again.

Chapter Five

The plan had been to go and deliver Sara's message to Steve then grab some food. Andrew was starving after the stress of everything that had happened at his parents' house. That plan had been fine in theory but now he was sitting in Sara's car outside the fire station and the prospect of walking into the big group of strangers seemed more intimidating. The large bay doors hung open and uniformed figures moved around inside the building. This was why he was good with computers. Computers didn't stare at him or make his palms sweat.

It was ridiculous to think everyone was staring at him. The men and women inside had much better things to do than stop and stare at a skinny geek with social anxiety.

But logic and commonsense didn't really help his nerves.

He forced himself to get out of the car and flinched when the door slipped out of his hand and slammed loudly. Yep, everyone was definitely looking at him now.

Andrew resisted the urge to run. Showing fear was like blood in the air. If he acted like prey then he was prey and, just like in the animal kingdom, prey didn't live too long.

Straightening his back, he hurried toward the open doors of the truck bay. A few people in firefighter uniform were scattered about inside, checking and cleaning equipment.

A tall, slim man with huge arms saw Andrew standing there looking awkward and put down the cleaning cloth and helmet he was working on. The fellow headed in Andrew's direction. "Speak."

Speak? Who the hell does this guy think he is?

Now that the man was closer, there was clearly a big size difference between them. Not as bad as with Steve but it made Andrew wonder if the town didn't just grow super giant firefighters. Even the women here were tall and strong.

"I'm looking for Steve. Could you tell him Andrew is here, please?"

"Excuse me?"

Okay, someone had an attitude problem.

Andrew realized he was looking at the ground so perhaps the man simply hadn't heard him. Talking to someone's shoes wasn't the best way to communicate.

"Steve? I'm Sara's brother and need to speak with him," he repeated as he looked up trying to fake confidence he didn't feel.

Andrew's uneasiness grew as the firefighter looked him up and down with clear skepticism. "You're related to Sara? You don't look anything like her. She's a fit piece."

Charming.

Andrew determined that it wasn't just him. The guy definitely had an attitude problem.

He was beginning to feel like a bug under a microscope. A really weird bug with a super tall and dumb-looking microscope. Hell, he'd be surprised if the guy could spell microscope.

Asshole.

They were starting to attract a lot of attention from the people in the truck bay. Andrew sensed every gaze as if they were pins in his skin. Why had he agreed to do this again?

"Yeah, tell me about it," he muttered, feeling anger slowly start to overtake his embarrassment. He should be accustomed to being weighed, measured and found wanting, but it still bothered him like an itch at the center of his back that he couldn't reach. "Steve?" Andrew pulled his superior computer guy persona around himself. He even arched a brow in question.

A second man in full gear walked over to join them and Andrew repeated his question. This guy was much friendlier and had a nice smile that reached his warm eyes. Next to the dark cloud beside them, it was the difference between night and day.

"Oh yeah, sure. Our team just came back from a shout so he's likely in the changing room. He mentioned you might be stopping by. Come on in."

The firefighter waved him through with another grin but Andrew didn't miss the lingering look of suspicion from Mr Dark Cloud.

"Thanks," he answered with a forced smile. "I'm Andrew. Steve is marrying my sister Sara." Since Steve worked with this guy, it was only polite to introduce himself.

"No problem. Steve's a good friend and is over the moon he's finally getting to marry your sister. They're great together. I'm Marty. Tell Steve I'm heading to the bunks for an hour," Marty said cheerfully.

Andrew could see the tiredness in the man now.

Marty gave him a wink and lead him in through a door and pointing down a small corridor before throwing a "See ya, Drew," over his shoulder and disappearing through another door.

Weird. But nice.

Perhaps it was weird *because* he was nice? Either way, it was heartening to see Steve had at least one good man at his back in case of a dangerous situation.

He strode quickly down the corridor until he spotted the door labeled Changing Room and headed toward it.

Through that door, Andrew found two more doors. One male and one female. For some reason he'd never thought of the intricacies involved with facilities in a fire station. He guessed he'd always just assumed there was a shared room but yeah, not very practical now he thought about it.

As luck would have it, Steve was standing at the lockers so Andrew didn't have to shout out or go searching for his friend. Steve looked up and grinned when he saw Andrew.

It was a nice welcome to say the least. Even better when in nothing but a towel Steve grabbed him into a hug. After nine years in the city, where you were considered overly friendly if you said 'good morning' to someone, it shocked Andrew to receive all these hugs. Especially when it was his brother-in-law-to-be who was still damp from the shower and had a relatively small towel around his waist.

Desperately trying to stop his body taking notice, he pictured smelly old gym socks. "Uhm. You do remember I'm gay, right? And you're almost naked."

Laughing, Steve let him go, slapping him on the back. That was definitely a straight guy thing. "Come on, man. I know you're not going to jump me or anything."

Andrew was glad one of them was so sure about that.

"Let me just get dressed then we'll head for some lunch in the break room." Steve whipped off his towel with a wicked grin.

Oh, dear God. Now Steve *really* was naked. If Sara ever got wind of this then he would never ever hear the end of it.

He swore his neck was going to have a permanent crick in it when he quickly looked away before his gaze dropped somewhere it shouldn't. Laughter was Steve's only response. Andrew flipped his friend off.

Sara was a bit of a perv when it came to Steve and men. The one and only time he'd let her take them to a gay bar she'd forced him to dance with Steve and he was so embarrassed he'd tripped over his own feet. But that hadn't stopped her from trying to get other guys to dance with Steve.

Thank God her husband-to-be thought her kink to see men grinding on her husband was cute. And Steve would obviously do anything to make her smile, so he'd danced with gay guys all night and had let her watch.

"So how'd it go at your parents? I know you were nervous."

"Oh, man. You would not believe the show you missed earlier. Your lovely bride hit Angela right in her pointy nose. I missed the actual punch but the aftermath was like a train wreck. I could *not* look away. My parents now know what kind of person Angela really is. Sara deserves some kind of a reward. She was awesome. I'm thinking I might buy her a giant basket of those mini muffins she loves from that bakery she always drags us to when you're in town."

"She didn't!" Steve sounded shocked and a little awed.

He also appeared a little turned on but Andrew really didn't want to go there.

"That's my girl," Steve said proudly. "I can't wait to go home tonight."

"Gag. That's my sister you're day dreaming about." Andrew didn't want to know what Steve and Sara got up to together.

Steve snorted but went back to drying himself and Andrew returned to looking anywhere else except at his friend.

"Go with triple chocolate and caramel. They're her favorite."

"Will do," Andrew agreed obediently.

In Andrew's peripheral vision, Steve ran the towel over his chest and Andrew knew his face was bright red as he kept his focus firmly on the ceiling. Counting the cracked corners of the foam ceiling tiles worked quite well. At least until a wet towel landed over his head.

Andrew wrenched the thing off with a growl and tossed it back at Steve but he missed and the towel sailed over his friend's head and landed with a wet plop. *Damn it.*

The sound of showers running in the background reminded him they weren't alone and that he couldn't kill Steve. Plus the man was kind of his best friend and it would suck not having him in his life.

Steve got dressed quickly then they were ready to go grab some food. A few firefighters had come and gone in the time Andrew had waited and he'd had to stop staring at the ceiling in case they thought he was contemplating putting a peephole in it.

Just as they reached the door, it opened and another enormous man stepped through it. *Do they only let genetically superior beings in here?*

In the doorway stood the most handsome man he'd ever seen — in his entire life.

Andrew was so busy admiring the newcomer that he didn't hear Steve talking to him until he was nudged and given a weird look. The man was at least six-foot-seven and had massive shoulders and biceps that stretched the navy T-shirt he wore to the absolute limit.

Andrew experienced the weirdest sense of recognition but he was certain he'd have remembered meeting this man before.

The fellow offered him a warm smile with perfect teeth and the most familiar dimple on the left side of his mouth. Sandy blond hair kissed the top of perfectly curved ears, the strands sticking up at odd angles, probably from a fire helmet. Eyes bluer than the whole damn Mediterranean Sea stared down at Andrew with shock and gave him an even stronger sense of *déjà vu.*

"Huh?" Andrew blurted.

Steve gave him the look again that told him they were going to talk about this later. "I said do you want to meet my groomsman?"

"Uh yeah, sure," he answered distractedly.

"Theodore I want you to meet—"

The man—Theodore—brushed aside Steve's introduction with one giant hand. "I know who he is, Steve. It's been a long time, Drew."

There was no mistaking that voice. Andrew might not recognize the body—and damn what a body it was—but no one could fake that voice. Rich, deep, and just the right note of sweet and sexy to make Andrew want to drop to his knees and find religion.

"Teddy?" he barely whispered but his reply was clear enough as the man's bright blue eyes widened in pleasure at the nickname. If Andrew thought Teddy had been big in high school it was nothing compared to how tall and broad he was now.

"Hey, how'd you know about his tattoo?"

Steve's question snapped him out of it and he looked between an uncomfortable-looking Teddy and a curious Steve.

"Ya know, the one of a teddy bear in the fireman's helmet. The guys rib him about it but he won't let any of us call him Teddy," Steve explained with a frown, glancing between them as if he were watching a tennis match.

Andrew's throat almost closed up.

He desperately wanted to see the tattoo Steve was talking about, because it sounded damn familiar. In high school, all of his books wore his signature doodle somewhere on the cover, hidden amongst the other scribbles unless someone knew what to look for.

At thirty, Teddy was four years older than he was, the same age as Angela, so they'd never shared any classes and had only been in the same school building for a few months. However, Andrew had gone to every one of Teddy's football games and spent time with him when Teddy used to come over to the house and wait for Angela to get ready for their dates.

Teddy hadn't seemed to mind. Andrew knew he'd been in love with Teddy since the very first time he'd seen the older boy smile.

Then Teddy had betrayed him. Betrayed him and hurt him so badly he still hadn't fully recovered from the mental trauma years later.

The reminder turned the warm glow of seeing Teddy into a shard of ice carving up his heart. He wouldn't be fooled twice. And this time he wouldn't be fooled by a killer smile and a pair of hypnotic eyes.

"We have to go," he snapped, not giving himself or Steve the chance to backpedal or invite Teddy— *Theodore* — to have lunch with them.

Luckily, Steve let himself be dragged away because Andrew had no chance at all of budging the man if Steve didn't want to move. By the time they got to his car, or rather Sara's car, Andrew was sweating bullets and shaking so much the keys slipped from his fingers.

"Drew. Andrew! Get in the other side. I got this," Steve encouraged, bending to pick the keys up.

He stumbled around to the other side of the car and all but collapsed into the seat. The door fell shut but he barely heard it over his pulse. Steve placed a hand on the back of Andrew's skull and guided his head down between his knees then massaged his neck a little.

He tried to control his breathing and get in sync with the one-two-three-four count Steve was chanting softly. Andrew guessed as a firefighter, his friend had seen his fair share of panic attacks.

The simple touch and silence slowly calmed him. Thinking of Steve and Sara having a baby to dote on, to love and cherish, and for him to spoil rotten, let Andrew get his panic back under control.

"You're going to be a great dad," he said, voicing his thoughts.

"Thank you. I hope I'll be as good a father as Sara will be an awesome mother. But don't you think you should explain what just happened in there? I've never seen you act that way before. It was like you were hit by lightning one minute and the next you were running away from your worst nightmare."

Sitting up, he swiveled to the side so he faced Steve. His friend immediately opened his arms and Andrew fell into them. This was exactly what he needed. Burying his face into Steve's neck, he tried to get a hold of himself.

"Hey. It's okay. You're safe," Steve murmured.

Safe. Geez. If only Steve knew.

Steve held him close for another minute or so before pulling away and making him face his gaze. "Are you ever going to tell me what's going on in that brain of yours?"

Seeing the depth of concern in his friend's face, Andrew knew he couldn't just brush him off or tell a half-truth. "Maybe sometime. But not right now, okay? Let's just say I was hurt badly before I left town by some people and leave it there."

"All right. But let me know if I need to have words with someone."

The big fellow kept Andrew's gaze until he nodded, message received. Steve had his back if he needed him.

Steve winked and flexed his muscles. It had the desired effect and Andrew couldn't suppress the burst of laughter. His humor doubled when a loud rumbling growl issued from Steve's belly and the man gave an embarrassed snort.

"I guess we best feed you before my sister finds out I've been starving you. You mind if we go somewhere instead of staying here?"

"That's fine. My team's on break until next shift change in an hour or so. Lead on, Drew. Genie's?"

He hadn't had Genie's cooking since her last visit. Even in the city there wasn't a chef he'd tried who could hold a candle to his sister's cuisine. "Sure. I'm buying."

"Of course you are. After seeing me naked, the least you can do is buy me dinner. What kind of slut do you think I am?"

"An annoying one," Andrew said, laughing again. He'd been in town for a total of twenty-four hours but he'd had more emotional ups and downs than a rollercoaster.

Chapter Six

Dinner was going to be on the table any minute and Andrew still hadn't managed to learn the identity of the extra place mat owner. Everyone else was here and assured him it wasn't for Angela. *But if not for her, then who?* And why was Sara looking like she'd swallowed a pinecone every time he brought it up?

Speak of the devil.

There was a knock at the door and his mother turned around from where she stood at the stove stirring the tomato sauce in a huge pot. Smiling, Andrew rubbed his stomach in anticipation. Mom's sauce was the best. It was clear where Genie had gotten her cooking talent. This sauce was awesome, though. Wars had been started over less. His mom always made a batch big enough to feed an army then doled out the majority of it between his sisters and now the firehouse.

"Get that, will you, Drew?" she asked and returned to stirring.

"Yeah, sure." He tried to convince himself it wasn't going to be someone horrible on the other side of the worn, wooden door.

Walking through the living room, he spotted Sara pointedly not acknowledging him and Steve looking really guilty, as if he'd just run over someone's puppy.

This is going to be bad.

Unable to drag out the six-foot walk to the door any longer, he bit the bullet and opened the door wide. As luck would have it, the sun was at just the right height in the sky to blind him so he couldn't see their visitor.

Clasping a hand over his eyes in the hopes of saving what was left of his retinas, he waved whomever it was inside and closed the door when he heard the person step over the threshold and move beside him.

The stranger was a glowing green hole in his vision. The glare cleared after a moment as his eyes adjusted and he saw the second worst person he could see. Theodore. *Teddy.*

All he could do was stare. Hell, he wasn't even sure he if he was breathing and blinking.

Why? Why is he here? Everything was just starting to turn around. He'd even finished having a conversation with his dad about computers where he'd agreed to teach him how to do stocks online. He should have known better. *Never feel safe because that's when the other shoe will fall on your fucking head.*

"Theo, son, glad to see you could make it," Andrew's dad said as he looked at them from the living room.

Steve and Sara had made themselves scarce. Genie, on the other hand, clearly wasn't in the loop either and greeted Theo warmly before rushing back to the kitchen.

Smiling widely, his dad walked to Theo and clasped the big guy's hand. It was clear the two men were used to talking by the way they stood close with their shoulders relaxed. "How's the house going, Theo? The old Jones house, right?"

Andrew was so angry he clenched his fist. He felt like a fool for trusting everyone. How could his parents do this to him? How could Sara and Steve? Okay, they didn't know exactly what went down on the night he'd left but they did know he hadn't talked about Ted — *Theo* — since.

Steve, and by association, his sister Sara too, knew how he'd reacted earlier when he'd seen the massive man mountain. So why the hell hadn't one of them warned him?

"I'm glad I could too. The house is fine, thanks. I've managed to get the first floor renovated and next I'm going to start on the roof while the weather holds steady. Thanks for inviting me, Drew," Theo said politely.

Teddy even had the gall to smile at him!

Clenching his fist harder, Andrew forced his words out. "It's Andrew now. And I didn't know you were coming." He kept his voice cold and unfeeling but it was no more than the traitor deserved.

"Drew! Why are you being so rude? He was your friend! At one point you two were nearly inseparable," his dad raged, upset and embarrassed by Andrew's behavior.

"The key word there is *was*, Dad. Some things just can't be forgotten." Switching his gaze to Theo, Andrew narrowed his eyes and struck Theo with a look he hoped was filled with all his hurt and betrayal. "Or forgiven."

Genie and their mother came out to see what all the shouting was about.

Without giving anyone else a chance to blame him for the situation, he walked away. He couldn't return to his hotel, because Genie was his ride back. And his sister had looked just as shocked as his parents had when he'd pushed past her to the staircase.

He paused at the top of the stairs. Perhaps he should have thought this plan through. Where was he going to go now? His room? Yeah, right. His mother had probably turned it into a craft room the second he was out the door.

Nevertheless, he found himself heading for his old sanctuary.

The door was the same, and although it had been covered in a coat of paint or two over the years, it still bore the same nicks and dents. He could still remember most of them happening.

There was a long slash-like dent where he'd experimented with skateboarding before realizing he barely had the coordination enough to walk in a straight line, let alone balance on a plank with wheels.

Next to that was a half-inch chunk of wood gouged out from the time he'd tried to learn archery and nearly killed himself with a damn arrow.

The one that drew his eye most, though, was the small half-moon scratches on the bottom edge of the door. He and Ted—Theo—had sat either side of the door when Andrew had caught a stomach bug that had been so bad he'd been in Mom-enforced quarantine.

Despite Angela's bitching and moaning, Theo had stayed with Andrew the entire time, talking to him and slipping him comic books under the door and only going home to sleep. Andrew smiled at the memory. He reached out and traced the marred wood with his fingers. It was one of his favorite memories when he let himself think of the past.

But like always, with the good there was bad.

Just above that and to the right there was a large dent in the door with veined splinters running up the grain. His suitcase had gotten caught the day he left and he'd been so upset he'd just yanked it free, damaging the door and not looking back.

He must have pressed too hard on the crack, as with a soft click, the door swung open. Curious to see what had become of his old room, he walked into it but came to a halt.

Andrew was at a loss as he walked inside. Everything was there. Obviously, someone had been in here to clean regularly but other than new curtains, everything was the same.

All his magazines and books were still in piles on his desk and the action figures and novelty ornaments were still exactly where they'd been nine years ago. The notice board he'd kept all his doodles on was still in two pieces where he'd broken it in a fit of anger and hurt. Every sheet and scrap of paper was stacked neatly on top of the two board halves.

It was as if he'd never left for college.

Or maybe his parents had thought he'd come back.

With a heavy heart, he plopped down on the end of his old bed. Why was everything so complicated? Before he'd come here, he'd been certain that his parents didn't care, Angela would get away with all the horrible things she had done and that Teddy had betrayed him.

And now, sitting in the room he'd spent all is childhood and teenage life in, he wasn't certain of any of it. If his parents didn't care then why keep his room and all his stuff the same?

Angela clearly wasn't going to get away with everything since Sara and Mr Robinson were giving their statements to the police and Mr Robinson's lawyers would file charges over the next few days.

Theodore—Teddy, or whoever the hell the man was—seemed confused and hurt by Andrew's reaction and attitude. So what was going on and why was everything turning upside down?

Buzzing distracted him from his thoughts and he realized his phone was ringing in his pocket. A quick look at the display let him know it was yet another person he didn't want to talk to—Martin, his supervisor.

Martin was pretty much a glorified babysitter. He was also the one Andrew thought was behind the shady deals and operations going down in his Intelligence section of the CIA.

Martin was not a person he wanted to sit and chat with over a cup of coffee, especially since he was technically on vacation and therefore not under jurisdiction of CIA supervision. However, Martin clearly wasn't the type to stress about rules.

Unable to avoid it, he clicked the answer sensor, held the phone to his ear—and immediately regretted it when Martin yelled over the line.

"What the hell do you think you're doing? You think you have the right to just take a holiday, fairy boy? You do what I damn well tell you to do and that's it!"

"Martin," he said calmly, trying not to show his irritation. This was not going to end well. "Martin, listen—Martin! I am entitled to vacation time allotted to me in the contract the CIA required me to sign."

"I don't give a shit what a worthless piece of paper says. You do what I tell you, when I tell you and I'm telling you to get your queer ass back here right now!" Martin was brusque and rude at times but this was beyond even the tensest encounters Andrew had ever had with the man.

Something was up.

"I can't do that, Martin. If you need a tech guy then I'm sure one of the other guys can handle it," Andrew hedged. His palms began sweating and the hairs on the back of his neck rose with unease.

"Don't you dare give me that shit. You think I don't know you've been snooping through my business. If you don't come back then—"

The sound of a throat clearing startled him so much his fingers slipped over the screen and an unmistakable beep signaled his hang-up. Damn. Glancing up to see who was at the door, he discovered it was the last person he expected to confront him.

Teddy.

Double damn.

He looked down at the phone. Wincing, Andrew could only imagine how angry Martin was now.

Despite the man's threats, Andrew knew there had been no evidence of his 'snooping' so it was just paranoia. But a paranoid CIA agent could be very dangerous.

Genie's friend better get back to town quick, because he had a feeling he was going to be having a visit from Martin in the near future. Shaking his head, he turned his attention back to the man currently at his door.

"What do you want, *Theo?*" He meant for the question to come out cool and aloof but even he heard the note of fear and neediness in his voice.

Theo shifted his weight from foot to foot and it should have looked ridiculous considering how big the man was but he just seemed vulnerable. It angered Andrew. What right did the man have to feel hurt? *He* was the one who'd been betrayed. *He* was the one who still had nightmares. Not Theo. Not *Teddy*.

"I came to see if you were all right and to apologize for whatever I did to upset you, then I heard your phone call and someone yelling at you. Is everything okay?" Theo actually managed to seem concerned.

It was funny. Andrew didn't remember Theo being much of an actor but the man was well on his way to earning an Oscar right now. "You seem concerned," he said with a sardonic smirk.

There was no way in hell he was going to let on how confused he was. Emotions like that were nothing more than weaknesses to be exploited when facing the enemy.

When they were friends, Andrew was an open book to Teddy. But that was then and this was now. Okay, maybe he was overacting a little. But he still didn't want Theo to know what he was thinking or feeling.

"I am concerned, Dre—Andrew. I don't know what I did to make you so cold toward me but I'm sorry. Whatever I did, I'm sorry," Theo pleaded.

All Andrew could do was watch as a tear tracked down over Theo's cheek, his eyes red-rimmed. Even the dimple looked sad.

This certainly wasn't the man Andrew remembered as someone who'd driven him away from his home. But he sure as hell wasn't going to take the chance of trusting whichever personality Theo was wearing today.

Andrew realized he was staring and hadn't answered when Theo came closer and dropped to his knees, putting them at eye level. When a big hand came toward his face, he couldn't help the instinctive flinch and raise of his arm as a shield.

When nothing happened, Andrew lowered his arm and looked back at Theo. The man seemed frozen and in complete shock. He wasn't even sure Theo was breathing. Theo's face started to go red as if blood vessels were bursting.

Swaying, Theo nearly fell to the side. Andrew had to put a hand out to steady the bigger man. If the Theo went down, he might do some damage, possibly even break bones because he was so big. Andrew forgot for a moment that he should fear Theo.

"Teddy, breathe!" Without thinking, Andrew sat forward and took Theo's pulse as he put his other hand on his friend's muscled chest. It had been years since his last First Aid course and he hadn't kept up the certification renewal, but some things he never forgot.

Theo's body obeyed his command and his chest immediately expanded and pulled in a lungful of air. His thready pulse was getting steadier with every breath, so Andrew figured it wasn't actual shock, just an *OMG* moment that tricked Theo's body into a reactionary shutdown.

"Just concentrate on your breathing for a minute," he said quietly before pulling away.

The second Andrew broke contact, Theo's head shot up and Theo clamped a hand over Andrew's wrist. Now Andrew was the one not breathing. They were inches apart and with no room to avoid looking into the blue eyes Andrew used to fantasize about.

"I wouldn't ever hurt you, Drew." There was no hint of a lie or deception in Theo's voice or in his beautiful face.

It was too much. All this—his room, his parents, his sister, his boss and the best friend who had betrayed him. Everything was confusing and not as it seemed.

Andrew broke Theo's hold before running from the room. Taking the stairs a few at a time, it was a miracle he didn't fall and break his neck. His mother stood at the bottom of the stairs and he couldn't bring himself to upset her after seeing his room so he pressed a kiss to her cheek, thanked her for dinner and stating that he had an emergency to take care of.

He was out of the house faster than he intended, the door slamming behind him so loudly he wouldn't have been surprised to hear his parent's neighbors complaining about it. By the time his sneakers hit the pavement, he was running at top speed.

All his teenage life he'd tried to find some hidden talent at sports, any and all sports, in attempts to impress Teddy. But he just wasn't good at any of them.

Three broken arms, four nasty sprains and almost all of his body having been bruised or scraped at some point later, Andrew had given in and accepted the fact sports weren't for him.

But his thin body seemed to be made to run.

He might not be a stickler for technique but the movement and clarity he got from running was unparalleled. Every morning and on summer evenings when the days were longer, he'd run the park circuit until his body had nothing left and his mind was clear.

It was a good five miles back to his hotel but he hadn't had a chance to run for two days and his body loved the stress relief. With every stride, his legs stretched and his muscles expanded and contracted until he fell into a familiar rhythm.

The scenery of the town flew past him as he continued his run. He passed his old school, the library, the computer café and didn't slow down.

There were a few nightclubs and trendy bars and there were one or two gay bars as well. The people here seemed to know everything about everyone else and most of the population was well-to-do and more concerned with materialistic gain and one-up-man-ship than disparaging sexual orientation.

People here would much rather dislike a person for what kind of car he or she drove or what sort of flowers someone grew than who they slept with. Especially since most folks here had enough of their own skeletons to hide about their sex life.

Andrew wasn't a big drinker. In fact, he hadn't ever had more than three alcoholic drinks at any one time. Even then, that was because his roommates at college had harangued him into going to a club. Seeing his friends completely out of control of their own bodies scared him away from alcoholic indulgence.

But right now, a drink sounded exactly like what he needed.

Chapter Seven

Two hours later, Andrew was drunk. Well, truly and officially drunk.

But the good news was that he felt great and everything that had seemed so overwhelming before was crystal clear. The painting of a duck wearing a sailor hat had helped him talk through things.

Funny thing, though, the barman didn't seem to want to talk to the duck. Some people were just rude. And now he was cut off.

"Hey, buddy. Where to?"

The barman called a cab and poured him into it as Andrew called goodbye to his duck friend. Rolling his head back on the headrest in the backseat of the cab, he gave the first address that came to mind when the driver repeated his question.

The only problem was that he was pretty sure it wasn't *his* address they were heading to. It was dark outside now and the streetlights glowed. If he looked at them just right, squinting and scrunching his face, the lamps looked like a continuous line of brightness.

Cool.

After a few minutes, or what seemed like a few minutes in his drunken state, the cab pulled up to a large three-story building. It was the old Jones home.

The house stood on about four or five acres of land before the closest neighbors could be seen. The Jones were an old couple who his mother said run off to a retirement home in Hawaii and left the house in disrepair before selling it off to someone.

Someone — he knew who it was — but he just couldn't seem to remember... *Uh-oh.*

Stumbling out of the cab, he fumbled in his pockets for his wallet. Shoving some bills at the driver, he figured he'd massively overpaid by the impressive wheel spin the cabbie managed as he sped away.

He was at the Teddy bear's house. Andrew wondered if Teddy liked porridge.

Why couldn't he be this funny when he was sober? The first sip of whiskey had tasted awful and almost made his ball sac shrivel up. But by the fourth, it was an exotic flavor scorching over his taste buds. Or should that be erotic?

And it gave him the clarity of mind to see things as they were and what he could do about them. He had to confront Teddy... Theo... Whoever the hell he was, and tell him why he was such a betraying bastard and demand that he stop looking so hot!

Now there was a good plan.

Bolstering his courage, Andrew stormed up the walk and pounded on the door.

Banging his fist over and over again against the wooden door made his head hurt but strangely he didn't feel a thing in his hand. Raising his hand so he could see it, he flexed his fingers.

Nope he didn't feel a thing. Huh.

He didn't have time to see if the numbness had spread to other parts of his body, as the door opened and a very sleepy and very angry-looking Teddy stood with a hand on the door as though ready to shut in Andrew's face.

"Who is it?"

"Hi, Teddy bear. Y'know I don't drink as a rule but five minutes in your copnamy... No *company*, and I'm totaled. But you know what else? I see things clearly now," he slurred.

"What? Drew?"

Apparently alcohol also allowed him to assert himself. Pushing past Teddy, Andrew found himself in the middle of a building site. Tarps lay everywhere over the furniture and the smell of paint still clung to the air a little.

"What is going on? Are you all right? Are you hurt?"

"Yes! Hurt, exactly! You hurt me. You let them... Why? Why didn't you help me? You said you'd keep me safe always then..." As quickly as his bottle of confidence had come, it left him.

Shaking and sobbing, Andrew sank to the floor and just cried out all the hurt and confusion.

Teddy slipped his arms came around him and didn't let go when Andrew fought them, so gradually he gave in and let Teddy hold him. It was better than being alone. His head throbbed, his heart pounded crazily and he was sure he was going to throw up soon.

Teddy moved his arms and suddenly lifted Andrew, who didn't have the energy to protest as Teddy carried him upstairs.

"It's okay, baby. I got you."

* * * *

Morning arrived and brought with it the mother of all migraines.

Andrew braved opening his eyes a crack and prayed he was in his hotel room. Or better yet at home, in his apartment hundreds of miles away.

Nope. No such luck.

Everything was blurry but he did notice a small bedside table within arm's reach and saw his glasses were neatly folded and placed on a cleaning cloth. There was also an unopened bottle of water next to them.

Andrew grasped the damn glasses and slid them into place. That fixed the blurriness. But it didn't let him recognize his surroundings.

Wherever he was had a comfy bed, nice warm magnolia walls, and a real fireplace. There weren't any photos or any books in the bookshelf on the left of the door, which was partly open, giving him a view of a spacious hallway.

Another door just to his left also stood open. It led to an en-suite bathroom. A big old-fashioned wardrobe stood on the other side of the room but if he had to guess, Andrew would say that it was empty too.

Andrew slowly eased into a sitting position and rubbed his temples in an attempt to get some relief from the ache in his head. He tried to stand and realized he was naked apart from his boxers. Did he do that himself?

He didn't think so since he always slept in a T-shirt and shorts.

As he stretched, his headache relaxed for a moment but before he could thank whatever god had taken pity on him, another ache started and he raced to the bathroom, pushing the door so hard in his haste it bounced off the wall.

He didn't have time even to close the door before everything he ate and drank yesterday came back up.

"Urgh." He hated puking.

Andrew was positive almost everyone promised this after a night out. His friends certainly did. But he was never, ever drinking again. It was evil stuff that made him think he was fine until it hit him right between the eyes.

Why the hell had he thought drinking would be the answer?

It was a stupid remedy and now he was in a strange place he didn't know, with God knows who. He was almost certain that huge chunks of last night were missing from his memory.

When he was finished, he pulled the lever, flushing the toilet, and crawled into the bath. The cool porcelain against his skin felt like heaven. Absolute heaven. Closing his eyes, Andrew just let the coolness sooth him.

He must have dosed off, because the next thing he knew, someone shook him and a shower of cold water poured over him.

"Fuck! Oh my fucking God!" Gasping for air, he clawed out at the hand holding him but couldn't move it.

"I don't remember you ever swearing this much. But then I don't remember you being a big drinker either."

A deep voice penetrated his state of shock.

Opening his eyes, he could just about make out a Theo-shaped blob through water droplets streaming over his glasses and into his eyes. "Theo?"

"So I'm Theo this morning but Teddy last night? You need to work on your morning-after etiquette.

Usually after you spend the night in someone's bed you aren't so formal in the morning," Theo joked with his signature-dazzling smile.

The water shut off and Andrew found himself smothered in a fluffy towel and being dried as though he was a child.

Theo was dressed in cutoffs and a baggy T-shirt, still looking like he could be on the cover of GQ.

Bastard, it just isn't fair.

"Let go of me," he snapped irritably, slapping at Teddy's hands.

Then Theo's words sank in and all the calmness left Andrew in a rush. "What! What do you mean, in your bed? We d-didn't—no. No," he spluttered, feeling way out of his depth.

Memories from last night of banging on Theo's door, yelling at him then being carried upstairs flooded his brain.

"Oh, God," he exclaimed.

Theo studied him for a minute as if Andrew was a puzzle he couldn't figure out. Then the man seemed to grasp what he'd said and why Andrew was freaking the fuck out.

"*No.* No, Drew. I'd never take advantage of you like that. You're safe with me."

"Yeah, okay." He laughed self-depreciatively. "That's what you told me before and look how that turned out, Teddy."

"You called me Teddy again," Theo commented, focusing on the wrong part of what Andrew had said. The man was infuriating.

"Yeah, I did. Sometimes I have trouble seeing who you are. Teddy was my best friend but he was also the one who hurt me. Theo is the grown up fireman, who apparently has no idea why I hate him."

Theo staggered back and away from him with a hand to his chest. The man seemed genuinely shocked. "You hate me?"

Suddenly very tired again, Andrew clutched the towel around him and ducked past Theo and into the bedroom in hopes of finding his clothes. "What did you expect after what happened?"

Theo followed him into the bedroom. Andrew sensed the man hovering behind him.

"What happened?" Theo asked.

"Oh, come on. The night I left early for college. Ring any bells?" Andrew knew he was being a bitch, but was Theo really expecting him just to brush it under the carpet? Or chalk it up to boys being boys.

Theo came to stand in front of him and put a hand on each shoulder to stop him from twisting away again. "Drew, I have no idea what you're talking about. But you're obviously upset about something."

Again, the lack of deception in Theo's face struck Andrew. The man he'd known was an awful liar and he couldn't believe he'd changed that much in nine years. But Andrew had been wrong before in judging people.

Andrew took a chance and let the towel fall away from him. He grasped Theo's hand. Very carefully, he brushed the other man's fingers over the most prominent scar on his chest.

Most of the injuries he'd sustained had healed on their own. And the others his roommate had slathered in antiseptic cream to prevent infection. Almost all of the marks had faded over the years except the one on his chest where Angela's jocks had held him down.

While Theo gently traced his fingertips over the rough, raised gouges left by fingernails, Andrew watched his face. He saw confusion, sympathy and a little anger but nothing else. There wasn't even a hint of recognition.

"You really don't remember, do you? The field, Angela and her jock squad, the football team?" He dropped his hand from Theo's in disbelief.

"Remember what?" Theo questioned. "Who did this to you? What they hell is going on, Drew?"

Andrew couldn't explain it but he believed Theo, which was insane when he thought about it. And he wasn't exactly running ten for ten on good judgment calls.

"I honestly don't know what you're talking about," Theo pleaded, looking desperate. He slid his hands up to cup Andrew's face.

Andrew's heart skipped a beat.

"The day after you left," Teddy stated, "I was in hospital with food poisoning and the doctors said I'd been hallucinating."

"I... I... I need to get d-dressed." Andrew was unsure where to go from here. This was possibly the only scenario he hadn't thought of when he'd considered confronting his former friend. And he'd spent a lot of time thinking when he'd first left.

He needed time to process, to get some sort of control over the situation.

Sighing, Theo released him and turned away but accepted Andrew's change of topic. "You're clothes stank like a brewery, so I threw them in the wash. They're not dry yet but I put a pair of my old sweats and a T-shirt on the bed when I heard you were up."

Andrew just watched as Theo headed for the door, looking like he'd just lost his best friend.

"Thank you, Teddy," he said.

Theo stopped but didn't turn around. "You're welcome, Drew. I'm due at the station in an hour, so

I'm going to take a shower then I'll cook some breakfast, if you think you can stomach it. The cold shower should have washed out most of the hangover but your body needs food."

"O-okay."

Andrew quickly dressed and sat on the bed until he couldn't put it off anymore. Gingerly, he made his way downstairs. Pans clattered about so he headed toward the noise, guessing that's where the kitchen was.

Theo was at the stove now dressed in his uniform, minus the flame suit. Next to him on the counter sat a plate of stacked pancakes but they weren't what Andrew was fantasizing about sinking his teeth into.

The navy shirt stretched tightly over Theo's impressive back and showed off the muscles that threatened to burst the shoulder seams. Andrew was a back man to be sure. There was nothing sexier than a muscled back flexing and contracting.

Theo's wide shoulders led to a slightly narrower waist with a seductive hollow just above his ass that Andrew could see from the T-shirt riding up. Then the *pièce de résistance*—a firm, tight ass carved out of marble from the gods.

Basically, the man was Andrew's walking, talking fantasy come to life.

Noise broke through his daydream and he managed to tear his gaze away from Theo's ass long enough to realize he'd been caught ogling. Oh, shit. Andrew just knew his face was brighter than the flames on the stove.

"Your phone is ringing, Drew," Theo told him, clearly struggling not to laugh.

"Uh, thanks." Fidgeting Andrew tried to fake some semblance of cool before turning and running in the direction Theo pointed to with a spatula. His ringtone cut off.

Just before he got out of earshot, he thought he heard Theo mutter, "So hot when he's flustered," but it must have been wishful thinking, or his imagination, because there was no way Theo had actually said that.

He spotted his phone and wallet on an old wooden side table in the next room and picked it up, quickly scrolling through his missed calls list. There were a few from Martin, one from Steve and two from Sara and Genie. Five from the hotel.

Hitting redial, he asked the receptionist—not Millie—why they were trying to contact him. She immediately put him on hold and instructed him to wait for a manager to speak to him.

Crappy elevator music blared down the handset, forcing him to lift the phone away from his ear to stop himself from going deaf. He glared at the screen in the hopes the person on the other end would feel it.

After a full minute of obnoxious disco tunes, a nasal voice came over the line asking him his name and room number.

"Now what is this about, please?"

The manager huffed and Andrew heard tapping in the background and guessed he didn't have the person's full attention. "I'm afraid we've had a report of a disturbance in your room and it is hotel policy to ask you to remove your belongings by five p.m. today—"

"What! I wasn't even in my room last night!" Waving his hands in the air as he spoke, Andrew tried to explain how it was impossible for there to have been a disturbance in his room last night.

"Please, sir, do not make this more difficult. Hotel policy about disturbances is clearly noted," the manager said sounding bored with the conversation.

Tough shit, he wasn't just going to roll over.

"Listen. You have electronic keys for the hotel, so you can just bring up the access schedule and see that I wasn't there!" This was ridiculous.

A disgruntled sigh followed by more tapping was his only answer. A minute later, the manager came back on the line and gave the same spiel of hotel policy.

"But you can see I didn't go back to my room last night!"

"I can see no such thing, sir. Your room key *was* used at exactly eleven twenty-three p.m. Please remove your belongings from the room before five p.m. today. Good day, sir." The bastard hung up.

This was a setup. It had to be. Throwing his phone down on the table, he then snatched his wallet up. There was no damn way someone used his room key because it was right here in his wallet. See, right—

"Shit!"

"Drew, you okay?" Theo came into the room, wiping his hands on a green hand towel.

Letting out a breath, Andrew tossed his wallet down next to his phone and leaned against the table. "Yeah, everything's good. Except someone apparently stole my room key last night and caused a 'disturbance', and now the hotel is kicking me out. And you know news like this travels fast around here, so there is absolutely no way I can just go and book into another hotel."

Theo dropped the towel and came toward him with a look of concern. "Someone stole your room key? Was it in your wallet?"

"Yeah. Why?"

Andrew watched as Theo picked up the wallet by the edges. Being careful not to touch it more than necessary, Theo opened it then checked his cards and money pockets.

"Everything else is there. It's just my room key missing."

"You have a black credit card and over a hundred dollars in cash but all they took is your room key? Doesn't that seem odd to you?" Theo asked with a look that clearly said Andrew should.

Now that it had been pointed out, the more Andrew was starting to think he'd been targeted instead of it being a crime of opportunity. It would have been much easier to take the cash and his card than leave them and take a chance on his room.

"It does now that you've pointed it out," he admitted, feeling stupid for not seeing it sooner. He worked for the CIA for goodness sake.

Theo placed the wallet back on the table and looked down at him. "We should call the police."

The thought of police digging around his life and through his stuff made his skin crawl so he quickly put a hand out on Theo's arm to stop him from heading for the landline phone.

"No. No police, please," he said nervously licking his lips.

Despite his obvious reservations, Theo relented. "I'll agree on one condition. You don't go back to your room alone. Wait for me to get off shift or ask Steve."

It wasn't an unreasonable request, and to be frank, Andrew wasn't in a rush to head back there despite the urge to check on his computer equipment. At least before he'd left his room he'd hidden his stuff under the bath, behind a loose board.

His equipment was worth a lot of money but more than that, his laptop was personal and had all his stuff on it and he wasn't about to risk it being nabbed by a sticky-fingered cleaner. Or a key-stealing burglar as the case may be.

"Okay. What time do you get off?"

Andrew chose not to look over the reasons he'd asked Theo to come with him instead of Steve. Just because Theo didn't seem to have any recollection of the attack didn't mean Andrew was over what happened. But Theo did make him feel safe.

However, he wasn't putting all his walls and guards down just yet, though.

"I finish at three," Theo said with a grin, looking like he'd just won first place in a competition. "Are you going to stay with your parents?"

"No, I'll probably go and bunk with Sara and Steve," he answered absently, thinking about whether he could convince his sister to let him sleep on their couch or, if he was lucky, the spare room.

He fiddled with his glasses before he could stop himself. Theo tracked the movement with a small smile.

"You know, you could always sleep in the guest room here again?"

Startled by the offer, Andrew stepped back. It was one thing letting Theo come with him to check out his hotel room but quite another to move in with the guy.

His surprise and panic must have shown. Theo took a step back himself and held his hands out in a non-threatening gesture. "I don't mean to push my luck, I swear. I just can't stand the thought of you running out of my life again. I still don't know what made you run or what scared you but please, please give me a chance."

Against his better judgment, Andrew realized he actually wanted to stay. He wanted to feel safe and cared for. He swallowed the lump of fear in this throat and nodded. "Okay."

Theo bounced a little. It was cute to see Theo so pleased that he was staying. It reminded him of when they'd hung out together and talked about films they were into. Despite the four-year age gap they'd had a lot in common.

"Can I ask one more thing before you remember how to say no?"

Andrew narrowed his eyes in suspicion as he saw a spark of mischief in Theo's blue ones. What was he up to? "What?"

"Will you call me Teddy?"

* * * *

Teddy headed for the station. Leaving Andrew alone, in his house, bored as hell.

Yes, Andrew had caved and agreed to call the man Teddy just to see that damn smile again.

But at least it gave him quiet time to think and process.

The couple of times Andrew had gone to see the college counselor/therapist/ headshrinker, he'd been asked if he thought not talking about what happened made him feel as if it hadn't. At the time, he'd scoffed and felt like he knew it all. Hell, at eighteen, who didn't feel that way?

But coming home had opened up a whole other can of worms. His family knew how evil Angela was, even if they didn't know about what she'd actually done to him. His parents, as it turned out, did love him and had been waiting for him to come home all this time.

And his sister and Steve had waited a long time for him to get his shit together so they could finally get married here. So much had changed from everything he thought he knew three days ago.

And Teddy... Well, Teddy was the biggest mindfuck of them all.

Andrew would have to figure out what to do about that sooner rather than later now that he'd agreed to living with the man while in town. He still had no idea why he'd agreed.

He glanced at the utensil clock on the kitchen wall and figured he had an hour and a half to kill before Genie picked him up to meet with her friend. Well, they actually had two hours but knowing her, she'd arrive early to grill him about why he was staying with Teddy after he'd treated the man like dirt at dinner. *Fun times.*

So now what to do?

He didn't know how to do anything DIY related so he couldn't carry on the house renovation. Plus he'd probably screw it up anyway. Andrew walked through the house as he looked for something to do. Teddy had said he could help himself to anything and even showed him where the spare key was.

Another overwhelming fact.

Teddy had given him free reign to snoop and poke about. The man's exact words as he'd headed out the door had been, "Snoop, poke about and feel free to go through anything you want. I won't be offended."

Teddy had handed him the proverbial keys to the kingdom. Best not to disappoint him. He smirked and let out a shout of laughter before running up the stairs. At the landing, he started making his way down the hallway, opening doors as he went until he found the master bedroom.

Unlike the room he'd stayed in last night, the bookshelves were full to the brim. Surprisingly there were many of the same titles in his own bookcase back home in his apartment. Mystery, crime, a few classic fantasy novels and some that Andrew hadn't gotten around to reading yet.

Putting the books back he'd picked up, he looked around the room. The bed, solid wood with carved headboards, matched a table. The room had a light and airy quality to it with the soft colors of the linens and walls.

Clearly Teddy had the decorating gene and that was rare for a straight man.

That thought hit him like a bucket of ice water. Teddy was straight and completely out of his league. But he was also once engaged to Angela so there was no accounting for taste.

Shaking his head in disgust at himself, Andrew turned to inspect the electrical stuff. A small but decent stereo and a little flat screen sat on top of a cardboard box labeled 'games'.

"Should I look?" Andrew fingered the closed lid of the box.

When he was a teenager, he'd had a habit of thinking aloud. He'd mostly been able to train himself out of it in college but sometimes, when he was stressed, the habit came back.

Of course he was going to look. It wasn't often someone gave you permission to rummage through their life. A beat-up PlayStation with a mess of wires that Andrew couldn't ignore lay in the box. He didn't look up from his task until the chaotic bundle of wires resembled the original packaging.

Opening the crate next to the one he'd just done, he went in search of games. Like books, one could tell a lot about a man by his games. He kneeled and dug in.

Thankfully, they were mostly classics like Crash Bandicoot alongside a few more recent releases. Andrew was a computer geek through and through and liked games as much as the next nerd. But in an oversaturated market of hack-n-slash trash, quality was sometimes hard to find.

"He can't be evil if he has Crash, right?"

Once he'd put everything back in the box, he got to his feet and wandered around the room some more. In the wardrobes, he found T-shirts neatly stacked and folded trousers and jeans. Even the man's sock draw was immaculate.

The Teddy he remembered would have laughed himself into a pulled muscle if Andrew had said he'd be this organized when he grew up.

Sitting on the bed, he tested the firmness with a little bounce. Comfy with just enough bounce to make things interesting with more than one person on the bed.

Not that Andrew would be getting any first-hand knowledge on being in or on the bed with Teddy. At least not outside of his own head.

He headed back downstairs and realized it was only the kitchen and the main sitting room that were finished. Tarps spotted with paint and various boxes of tools covered everywhere else. There were different electric saws, drills, a few hammers and countless tubs of assorted nails and screws neatly stacked in each of the rooms on the ground floor. Teddy probably had a few men from the fire station chipping in to help with the work so it made sense to have several drills and hammers and such.

On his second circuit around the house, he spotted some boxes filled with electrical wires and a much bigger flat screen than the one upstairs. "Now this is more like it," he said smiling.

This was something he could work with.

Chapter Eight

Genie was due any minute to pick him up for the meet with Agent Christopher Hammer, and Andrew was officially out of things to do. He'd installed the television and hooked up the cable with free limitless channels, of course.

The computer was set up and the highest speed Wi-Fi connection available throughout the house and he'd even managed to configure an adapter for the garden out of bits and pieces he'd found on his scavenger hunt around Teddy's home.

The only thing he hadn't done was go through Teddy's computer files, because his conscience drew the line there, considering all the private information he kept on his own computer.

Almost everything electrical could now be run from a reconfigured universal remote he'd found and rewired.

He got bored quickly.

Whether Teddy would actually appreciate his meddling was yet to be seen. But he wouldn't have long to wait since the man in question was due home in a few hours.

There was that pesky use of the word 'home' again. This wasn't his home and he needed to remember that.

Bouncing his leg, Andrew tried not to keep checking the clock. Perhaps he had time to look through the computer after all. It sat on the old desk by the bay window, looking at him. His fingers twitched with the very powerful temptation.

Saved by the bell.

The old-fashioned bing-bong of the doorbell rang through the house and he shot up off the worn leather sofa to answer it. When he opened the door, he expected to see Genie waiting there impatiently and ready to jump on him with a million questions.

"Hi, Ge—"

Instead, he came face-to-face with a man dressed in jeans and a casual cotton shirt. The man wasn't overly tall but something about the way he stood with a pinched expression on his face urged Andrew to gulp and step back. This man was dangerous.

"Chris, stop scaring my brother with your crazy-person look." Genie's voice came from somewhere behind the stranger. Elbowing the man out of the way, Andrew's sister came forward and drew him into a hug.

"Sorry for last night. I swear I had no idea what was going on between you and Theo," she apologized.

When he pulled back to give her a questioning look, she blushed and fussed with the strands of hair that had fallen from her ponytail. "Sara, told me about how you used to have a crush on Theo and how upset you were when Angela announced they were engaged before you left town."

Well, that answered the questions as to how much Sara knew. Some, but by no means all. He'd found out a month or so after he started college that Angela hadn't actually told Teddy that Teddy and her were engaged.

According to Steve, who he'd called after he'd finished setting up Teddy's electrical equipment, Teddy had refused to speak to his sister after Andrew had left town.

It was hard not to smirk at the reminder.

"Yeah, I was a bit upset. But that's not why I left you know," he felt the need to point out. Andrew may be the little brother but he didn't want his sister thinking he'd left just because his feelings were hurt.

Genie smiled a little as she caught his meaning and nodded. "I know, little brother. Someday you'll tell me what really went down that night but I think you have someone else to tell first, no?" She gestured at the borrowed clothes he'd forgotten he was wearing.

"Uh, speaking of telling someone something. Do you mind inviting us in so I can hear about your information, or do you want to remain a sitting duck for anyone watching?"

The gruff chastisement from the stranger made Andrew flinch but he stepped back and waved them inside.

"I thought we were meeting your friend at the restaurant." He glared at the man.

Christopher just met his glare with the cold detachment that Andrew imagined a serial killer would possess.

"I know. I'm sorry. Christopher suggested that it might be better to meet somewhere private to talk considering the... Sensitivity of the information..." Genie seemed worried.

It wasn't her fault he was up a certain creek without a paddle.

His sister patted his arm and gave Christopher a glare of her own that had little effect. Christopher scraped a hand over his buzz cut. "Sorry. It's been a rough couple of days."

"No worries." He accepted Chris' apology. A rough couple of days? That made two of them.

Andrew led them to the sitting room and motioned for them to sit. Genie took the sofa and Christopher sank in the armchair opposite the chunky coffee table.

"Do either of you want anything to drink?" It was weird playing host in someone else's house but the manners his mom had driven into him demanded he offer refreshment.

Genie stood again. "I'll go find the kitchen and make some coffee. You two sit and…talk," she said in a rush.

Before either of them could answer, she was gone.

"I don't think she wants to hear about the shady side of the CIA. I wouldn't hold my breath on getting that coffee any time soon," Christopher told him with a smirk. "So what's this information you think you have?"

Grinding his teeth at Chris' mocking tone, Andrew took a deep breath and reached for his phone. "I don't *think,* I know. I was recruited by the CIA as a hacker. My supervisor Martin Joseph Gimble has been jumpier than usual and more paranoid too. Some of the high-clearance operations have collapsed on the Intelligence end at the last minute. There is no way the targets could have known they were under surveillance with as much accuracy as they had."

At the mention of operations failing, the agent sat forward on the edge of the seat and leaned toward Andrew. "What do you mean?"

At least he had the man's interest now.

"First tell me exactly how you can help," Andrew demanded while he had the upper hand.

Christopher shot him a look of equal parts respect and annoyance, but Andrew didn't back down. This wasn't information he could just go around sharing with any average Joe. Yes, he'd given his sisters the bullet points but there was nothing concrete or dangerous for them. It was no more than a conspiracy believer could find on Google at this point.

"The company I worked for is an independent watchdog if you will. We deal in uncovering corruption and leaks in the intelligence factions and capturing the guilty party. Anything else you want to know? Shoe size, IQ or dick length?"

The crudeness of the question verbally slapped Andrew back. Angry and embarrassed, he grimaced as his cheeks heated. "No. I don't care about your shoe size, and your IQ probably rivals that of a houseplant. And your penny dick is none of my concern," he shot back.

Andrew may not be much to look at but the other man had made it personal when he implied his information was bogus.

Before he'd come home, he would have never dreamed of answering someone like that but he'd had enough of being pushed around. And to be honest, it felt damn good to stand up for himself.

What the hell had Genie seen in this jerk anyway?

Sure, the man had an asymmetrical face and he supposed some might find him handsome but his personality needed work—a lot of work. His sister could certainly do better.

A loud laugh startled him out of his thoughts and he realized he'd just been played. The harsh coldness of before vanished and Agent Christopher actually appeared friendly. When the man smiled, he was stunning.

"Penny dick? Now that's one I haven't heard before." Christopher chuckled.

"Yep, because that's all it's worth." Andrew allowed himself to laugh too.

Christopher slapped his knee and let out a big belly laugh. They sat for a few seconds and Andrew relaxed a little as his nerves settled.

"Sorry for the hard time. I just wanted to make sure you were doing this for the right reasons and had a backbone hidden somewhere behind the glasses and ringlets. Now back to why I'm here."

Reaching into his pocket, Andrew pulled his phone out. It was just a simple touch screen but with a few modifications, he'd made to it so he could access any and all of his files from any of his other devices.

As far as security went, the phone required a password and fingerprint recognition to unlock the screen in case it was ever stolen. To access those files there was a timed touch pattern the user had to enter in order to stop the phone from erasing itself.

Using his cell, Andrew connected to his laptop and opened the file that had all the information about Martin and the suspected information leaks, and passed the phone to Chris.

His stomach clenched with the aftermath of last night's drinking and the sudden stress of having a stranger look over all the evidence he'd gathered about a CIA traitor. Andrew hoped Teddy had some antacids somewhere.

"Well this is more than I expected. This is the smoking gun. Does this Martin know you have all this information?" Christopher asked shrewdly, his eyes sharp.

Andrew shrugged and palmed the back of his neck, trying to ease the tense muscles. "He thinks he knows but there is no way he can track me tracking him."

Agent Christopher stood up and passed Andrew his phone. "That doesn't mean he's not dangerous. Can you send that file to a secure server if I give you the codes?"

He bit back the sarcastic remark that a goldfish could do that. "Yes."

From the twist at the corner of Christopher's mouth, his unsaid comment didn't go unnoticed.

"Good. Now exactly what has Martin done to you since you came here? Genie told me in the car ride over that your other sister's fiancé Steve said his friend Theodore mentioned someone stealing your room key," Christopher recited like a well-learned script.

It took him a minute to decipher the train of thought but once he did, he rolled his eyes. Firefighters gossiped more than teenage girls did in high school.

"Yeah. Teddy made me promise not to go back to the hotel room without him. Whoever it was hasn't found my laptop," he stated with certainty.

Looking intrigued, Christopher cocked his head and asked with a suspicious tone, "How do you know if you haven't been back there?"

A long and detailed explanation followed about the various trackers he'd placed in his equipment to inform him via his cell if they were turned on or even moved without disabling the trackers.

Andrew just picked up his mobile and held it up with a grin.

Christopher looked suitably impressed. "We may have to talk about your proclivity for tracking things. I might have a job offer for you by the end of this. Listen to your friend Theodore and take precautions to stay safe. I'll be in touch. Tell Genie she was right."

Standing, Chris handed him a scrap of paper.

Glancing down at it, Andrew saw it was a sequence of codes. If it was for the secure server, it had some extraordinary levels of security.

"Is this—" Looking up, he found he was talking to thin air. The sound of the front door closing made him jump and spin around. By the time he got to the door and flung it open, there wasn't any sign of the man.

How the hell did he do that?

Genie's voice behind Andrew startled him. She ushered him back inside and shut the door. "He does that. Chris told me to stay with you until Teddy gets home."

"Going to protect me, big sister?"

"You know it." Genie winked.

Despite the joking tone, a certain glint in her eyes made him think he wasn't too far off the mark. She moved her right hand behind her back in an almost subconscious gesture. Andrew narrowed his eyes at the action. What was she hiding?

Genie pushed her hair back behind her ears unable to meet his gaze. "Let's go have that coffee now, huh?" Clearly she wanted the topic dropped. Exactly how much time had she spent with Agent Christopher Hammer?

Slowly, he nodded. "Yeah, okay. What were you right about anyway?" He guessed his sister had been eavesdropping.

"That curly brown hair and glasses were exactly his type. Too bad you're taken now, though. You two would have made a cute couple."

"I'm not taken," he protested, cheeks flaming.

His sister didn't say anything, just gave him a knowing look and headed toward the kitchen, leaving him to trail behind.

"I'm not!"

* * * *

Teddy came through the door at exactly twenty-five minutes after his shift had ended. Since the station was a good half hour away, Andrew had the feeling Teddy had been in a hurry to come home. Andrew would never admit to anyone the rush he felt at that thought.

He heard keys drop into a glass bowl then Teddy appeared in the entryway of the sitting room.

Teddy took one look at the room and smiled. "So you've been busy."

Ignoring the way his cheeks heated, Andrew toyed nervously with the arm of his glasses. "I set up your TV and computer so you don't have to do anything with them and everything runs off grid so it's free too."

Teddy raised his eyebrows and a frown creased his model good looks. "Free? Is that legal?"

Andrew let out the breath he'd been holding.

He stood and gestured at the TV. "It's legal but something the cable companies don't want you to know about. I put Wi-Fi throughout the house and the patio out back as well," he added.

"Thanks." Teddy slowly came toward him.

Unable to move, he stood frozen to the spot as Teddy came to a stop in front of him. His heart skipped a beat before running double time when Teddy pressed a kiss to his cheek.

"Thank you, Drew."

Andrew didn't know what to say so he just nodded.

When Teddy moved away, Andrew could breathe again. He was even starting to like being called Drew again.

This was dangerous territory.

"Looks like you boys are getting along fine today," Genie said in a tone Andrew couldn't quite identify.

He'd completely forgotten she was here.

"Since you're home, Theo, I have to get back to the restaurant. Hopefully there haven't been any disasters in my absence."

"Thanks, Genie…" There just wasn't a right word for everything. He'd have to get her a gift to say thank you.

"No problem, bro. Now go get your stuff so you can move in with your man."

"He's not my m—" It was no use. She was already out of the door.

With her departure, it left just him and Teddy. Alone with a straight man his sister had made clear his family thought he was dating.

Glancing at the fireman to apologize for Genie's teasing, he spotted Teddy wearing a grin so wide he could see all of his pearly whites.

He was so distracted staring at Teddy's Cupid lips that he forgot what he was going to say. *Damn, I'm sunk.*

"Drew?"

"Hmm?"

Teddy really was physically perfect. His mother used to say a strong jawline made for an honorable man. Teddy was certainly that—a lifesaver and good man. And Andrew didn't want to do anything to compromise that.

But how could he reconcile what he thought and felt about Teddy with what he remembered?

"Let's go get your stuff. Then we can talk," Teddy added with a note of trepidation.

Swallowing past the lump in his throat, Andrew agreed.

* * * *

"Explain to me again why you need so much computer stuff?" Teddy carried Andrew's bags in from the car and put them on the dining room table they'd brought in from the garage before they'd left.

"That computer stuff, as you put it, is my entire life. And my job too." It hadn't taken long to clear out his room but he'd also demanded to see the security CCTV footage. The manager clearly wasn't happy to help despite the notice on his name tag.

After Teddy had pointed out that it would be bad press for the hotel if people found out about the break in, the manager caved and had reluctantly cooperated. Word of mouth in a town like this was a powerful thing.

Teddy said that if the manager was so sure it was Andrew who had entered the room last night then he shouldn't have a problem handing the tape over.

Obviously, it wasn't the approach the manager had expected and he'd clicked his fingers for Miss Hair

Extensions to fill out the forms and have the tape delivered to Teddy's address tomorrow morning.

On the way home, Teddy had badgered him into spilling some of his secrets. It wasn't as though he hadn't expected it, since he was pretty sure most people didn't have to hide their stuff behind wooden boards under the bathroom sink.

To say Teddy had been surprised by his vague and hole-ridden story, of not being a tech but working for the government, was an understatement.

They'd actually pulled over to the side of the road where Teddy had spent the next ten minutes staring at him and firing questions left, right and center.

"So you're some kind of super computer guy but you can't say any more about it right now?" Teddy surmised, looking underwhelmed with Andrew's refusal to explain more.

When they'd gotten back to Teddy's house and set up his equipment, he'd told Teddy what everything was and a basic version of each piece's purpose. But Teddy surprised him again and was a quick study. Andrew bet Teddy could set all this stuff up on his own next time.

"Seriously, though. If you've told your sisters then you'll have to tell your parents at some point, because you know none of you can keep a secret to save your lives," he shot back.

Andrew could have pointed out he'd kept it secret for years but he was having too much fun going along with the conversation. Sticking his tongue out at Teddy, he laughed when Teddy clutched a hand over his heart as if he was wounded, feigning shock.

What had he done without Teddy to make him laugh?

A chime from his laptop reminded him to log in and disable the tracker. When the home screen came up, a small folder in the top left corner caught his eye and his humor faded.

Sitting down on the wooden chair, Andrew remembered exactly why he hadn't had this with Teddy for so long.

Teddy caught the change in his mood and immediately came over to him and crouched next to the chair. With a hand on Andrew's knee, Teddy offered him comfort without asking any more questions.

"I... I think I need you to watch something. This might be the easiest way to explain... Everything. Will you watch?" It wasn't a small thing he was asking.

The few times he'd gone to the college counselor, he'd agreed to have the sessions taped. It was as though the counselor had known he wouldn't be able to hack it for long. So now he had a home video of his pain where he'd rehashed everything and bared his soul to a stranger.

Andrew stared at the video file icon. Every little thing, every fear and scar was in those files.

But was he brave enough to let Teddy see them? There was no way he'd be able to get through talking about it face-to-face.

Just the thought of watching Teddy's face while he told Teddy was making him queasy enough that he had to push a hand to his stomach.

"Whatever you need me to do, okay? I know I'm missing something. And I have dreams—" Teddy cupped Andrew's face.

Teddy's gaze bored into his and Andrew saw the man was one hundred percent serious. But something else overshadowed his crystal blue eyes—fear?

Teddy broke their eye contact, clearing his throat.

It was Andrew's turn to seek out Teddy's gaze and offer comfort by placing his hands over Teddy's and rubbing his thumb over Teddy's knuckles.

"When I was in hospital," Teddy began, "the doctors said I kept crying your name. And after... I had bad dreams, dreams of you being hurt and not being able to stop it."

Okay, it didn't take a genius to make a connection between the dreams and what had happened. Would it do more damage than good if Teddy watched his files?

Yes, he'd have the closure of Teddy knowing how he felt about what happened but would this open up deeper wounds that neither one of them were equipped to deal with?

Andrew was desperately trying not to think about Angela's newfound hobby of drugging people. But the voice in the back of his head kept pushing it forward. He felt he owed it to Teddy to give him a choice.

Even if it meant putting his own trauma aside.

He'd had years to deal with it and he still had nightmares and panic attacks like the one that had struck him at his parents' house. Andrew wouldn't wish those on anyone, especially someone he had feelings for.

"You... Y-you don't have to watch them. I'm just glad you're back in my life," he explained, trying to convince himself as much as Teddy.

Teddy saw right through him, though. "Tell me honestly you don't need me to do this, don't need me to know whatever is on those files and I won't watch them."

Steeling himself, he took a breath and said with only a slight stutter, "I don't n-n-need you to watch them."

Teddy smiled but there was nothing funny or happy about it. Gently, he pulled Andrew out of the chair and pushed him in the direction of the stairs. "I'll be up when I'm finished."

* * * *

Staring up at the ceiling in Teddy's room, Andrew wondered if he'd done the right thing. He'd said some awful things about Teddy in those sessions.

Once Teddy knew everything, would he hate him?

Will I lose Teddy all over again?

The part that stuck out in his mind the most was the bit at the end of all four sessions. At the first three appointments, he hadn't answered the question the counselor had repeatedly asked him, but the last time he'd gone, the floodgates had opened. And he knew it was going to hurt the man downstairs.

"What would you say to Teddy if he with us now?"

"I'd say that I hate him for what he did. I'd say 'I loved you with everything I had and you used it to break me. You were there! You sat there and watched as they... How could you?'"

He'd cried for the rest of the session then spent days in his room just staring at the wall.

And he'd never gone back to counseling. He hadn't even looked at the files the counselor had sent him after he didn't show up for his next appointment.

Online, he'd read that sometimes trauma caused a sort of fuzziness or amnesia surrounding the actual incident. But that's not what he'd found. Like it or not—and he most definitely did *not*—he could remember everything up until he'd lost consciousness.

It had been the beginning of summer and he had just finished his last few exams and assignments. He remembered being so excited that he could spend time with Teddy and help him train for firefighter tryouts. Well by help, Andrew had meant carry water and watch from the sidelines. But it was still time with Teddy. Despite their age gap, they were the best of friends, much to the annoyance of his sister Angela, who kept trying to get into Teddy's pants.

He'd been stretching so he could go on a run while there was still light outside. He had just discovered that running was something his gangly body could actually do well and he was hoping it would build up some muscle definition.

Angela had come running up the walk, looking upset with her makeup running down her face. "Please, you have to come. There's been an accident. Theo's hurt," she cried, clawing at his arms and trying to pull him away from the house.

The year before, he'd taken a first aid course. He'd tried to get his phone out to call nine-one-one, but his sister had hit the cell out of his hands and screamed there wasn't time. In hindsight, that should have been his first clue.

Despite it being a small town, it possessed a lot of powerful people and the emergency services were topnotch. And he'd never seen his sister cry for someone other than herself.

Back then, he hadn't asked questions. He'd run to the kitchen and grabbed the first aid box from under the sink then followed Angela. When they'd reached the end of the street, one of her friends had pulled up and offered them a ride.

Another clue he'd overlooked in his panic over Teddy being hurt.

But they'd driven out to an unused field and he'd leaped out of the car in his hurry to get to Teddy. This particular field had been used only during hot summers where grazing ground was scarce and hadn't been cut yet.

His sister had led him through a path in the long grass until they got to a small clearing.

Teddy sat on an old car seat someone had obviously ripped out and dumped. He didn't even look Andrew's way. Andrew never got the chance to see if his friend was okay, because he was jumped from behind.

Whoever attacked him had slammed his head into the hard ground repeatedly until warm, wet stickiness dribbled down into his eyes and his face was on fire.

His attackers turned him over onto his back. Fingers dug painfully into his chest. He'd tried to get free. He'd cried and screamed for Angela to run and for Teddy to help him.

And that's when he'd heard it—a sick, twisted cackle from beside him. Someone suddenly lifted him to his knees. Angela stood with three more guys he recognized from the football team.

Or rather, the ones who *had been* on the football team during Angela's senior year. And they'd been in and out of the house over the years, her sleeping with at least one of them at any given time.

"Angela?"

His stomach clenched as he remembered how scared he'd been when she'd just laughed again and waved her left hand at him.

"Well, my little faggy brother, what did you expect? Me and *Theo* are going to be getting married soon and we don't need you panting after him down the aisle. So now you're going to get what you deserve. You're going to be my boys' bitch," she taunted while playing with the new ring on her left hand.

Before he could struggle or do anything more than scream, the men with her and the one still holding him started ripping at his clothes.

When he was naked, they had dragged him, kicking and shouting to an irrigation pipe that jutted a few feet out of the ground.

The football players ignored his pleas to let him go as well as the bargaining that no one would ever know what happened there if they'd just leave him and Teddy alone. Over and over, he called Teddy's name, but he got no response.

Teddy just stared as though he hadn't even heard him.

The ex-players had tied Andrew to the pipe with their belts and moved back. At first, they just looked at him, their eyes lighting up with a sick hunger.

For a moment, he thought this was it, just some humiliation and a broken nose then Angela came forward with a big bag.

Inside the bag had been some footballs. The ex-players had taken it in turns, kicking the footballs at him.

One after another. For what seemed like hours.

They kicked the balls at his face, his ribs, his groin, and almost every single one connected with force far exceeding a fist or a boot.

Andrew had thrown up from the pain but even that wasn't enough for them. The men had surrounded him and proceeded to jack off, covering his naked and battered body in their ejaculate.

He remembered how his throat had been too raw to cry or scream and that he'd tried to disconnect somehow with what was happening, but the pain had kept him grounded in reality.

Eventually, he'd lost consciousness and, when he woke up, he was untied but still naked and abandoned in the field. Somehow, he'd walked the six miles home and by good luck or not, everyone was out.

His parents were no doubt at a business dinner and his sisters had had places of their own.

Within an hour, he'd packed a bag and called a taxi to take him straight to the airport. He'd been prepared to pay the several hundred dollars fare but the driver had taken a last look at him, shook his head and said, "No charge. Good luck, kid." It hadn't taken much to persuade the university to allow him early admission since his computer science pre-test had led to a prototype system that would eventually save them hundreds of thousands of dollars.

So he'd left and had never come back.

Until now.

Coming back to the present, Andrew didn't know how much time had passed but suddenly he was aware of someone watching him. He didn't sit up, just waited for Teddy to say something or tell him to leave.

Instead, the mattress dipped before Teddy wrapped his thick arms around Andrew and cuddled him close to Teddy's solid, warm chest.

Teddy pressed his soft lips pressed against Andrew's ear as he whispered brokenly, "You loved me. I'm so sorry I didn't help you. I swear I didn't know. So sorry."

The last of Andrew's barriers fell and emotions overwhelmed him that were too ragged and unstable for him to put a name to them.

He didn't know how long they lay there. Gradually, he was so exhausted from crying that he fell asleep.

Chapter Nine

Waking up with the unfamiliar smell of sweat and smokiness was strangely comforting. He stretched but something held him still.

Andrew snapped his eyes open as he came immediately wide-awake.

His breathing grew short and shallow as panic built in his chest. He couldn't get free.

"Shh, baby. It's only me."

Before he processed that he knew the voice, his body calmed and his heart rate returned to normal.

Andrew pushed against the arms holding him just enough to turn his head and look at the man behind him. Teddy didn't open his eyes but Andrew knew Teddy knew he was watching him. The barest hint of a smile tweaked Teddy's lips as he tightened his arm around Andrew's waist.

Andrew nearly swallowed his tongue when a hard ridge pressed against his ass. That couldn't be what he thought it was. There was no way straight, heterosexual, women-loving Teddy was gay.

There was just no way. Sure, they'd slept together. But cuddling was a far cry from sex. At least he thought it was.

Perhaps Teddy just needed to piss.

Licking his lips, Andrew's cock hardened. He was really starting to wish he'd undressed before falling asleep.

Even though he was still in Teddy's baggy sweats and T-shirt, the excess material had bunched up underneath him, pulling everything tight at an odd angle. And Teddy was like a furnace behind him, overheating him.

"Teddy?"

For a moment, Andrew didn't think Teddy was going to respond. But then Teddy moved forward, and Andrew nearly swooned when Teddy pressed a couple of kisses to Andrew's throat.

"Go back to sleep, it's early," Teddy said.

Unable to stop himself, he let his head fall back to the pillow and got a nibble just behind his ear in reward. After several more sleepy kisses to his neck, Teddy lay back again and snuggled into their shared pillow.

There was no way the man was going to actually go back to sleep. No way.

Teddy let out a contented sigh and his breath evened out and tickled into Andrew's hair. Bloody hell he was. The man pulled Andrew closer, rubbing against his ass.

Andrew tried to hold in his groan and stop his hips from pushing back ever so slightly but his body was too aroused at the feel of Teddy's erection against him. He just prayed to whatever god was listening that Teddy didn't notice.

Even though he knew he shouldn't be doing it and he was terrified of getting caught, Andrew let his hand creep from his side, sliding it over his stomach.

He hesitated.

Andrew took a breath and, with an uncharacteristic loss of control, he pushed the waistband down and took himself in hand.

He stoked himself and gasped. Pre-cum leaked from the head of his heavy member and he swelled even more as he thought about Teddy pressing against him. He'd never been this hard and wanting.

Biting his lip, Andrew felt himself getting closer. It had been so long. No one besides Teddy had seriously turned him on. He could appreciate a handsome man but no one got his motor running.

Even his own hand hadn't been enough to get him off the last few months and he'd buried himself in work. But now, with Teddy pressed against his backside, there was nothing he could do to stop himself from pumping his cock until he came.

Andrew moved his hand faster as he dared to push back against Teddy again. Every time Teddy's shaft rode along his ass, a thrill shot through Andrew. It felt naughty and dirty and exactly what he needed.

At the final second, his conscience made him pinch off the pleasure at the base of his cock. No, this was wrong. Teddy was asleep, for fuck's sake.

Teddy had held him all last night, keeping the nightmares at bay. And it seemed wrong to take advantage of the sleeping man by beating off next to him.

"Don't stop now, baby," Teddy urged.

Teddy's voice startled Andrew into letting go of his cock. Without his hand in the way, the waistband of the sweats snapped back to Andrew's waist, crushing his abused erection.

"Ow! Fuck," he whined pitifully, holding himself.

Andrew tried to roll away. Now that he'd been caught, he couldn't believe what he had just done. What the hell had he been thinking?

He continued to try to get away until he realized Teddy wasn't actually yelling at him. In fact, it wasn't until Teddy moved Andrew's hands out of the way that Andrew realized that one, he was still hard, and two, so was Teddy.

His brain function fizzled out for a second. Teddy, his Teddy, the straight, sex-on-legs fireman was touching his dick and nothing else in the world existed.

All he could do was gasp. "Oh, my God."

Teddy pushed the sweats down again before taking hold of Andrew's cock as if he owned it.

Teddy played him. It seemed as though he knew Andrew's every secret turn on. He used just the right amount of pressure and the slightest wrist twist as Teddy reached for Andrew's cock. It only took a few strokes before Andrew was begging Teddy to let him come.

"Tell me how," Teddy demanded.

"Please talk to me. God, I could go just from your voice," he wailed, thrusting into the strong, calloused hand around his cock.

"Then that's exactly what you'll do." Teddy released Andrew's erection.

The only contact between their bodies was Andrew's back to Teddy's front.

Andrew tried to chase the delicious feeling of grinding his ass against his friend's jean-clad erection, but Teddy held him still. Andrew moaned at the loss but Teddy just laughed and kissed his neck.

"I missed you all those years you were gone. I didn't know what had happened before but I was waiting for you to come back for holidays or term breaks but you never did. I waited for you to be old enough so I could ask you out. I've loved you from the minute you fell down the stairs at my feet. I love you, and I want you to come for me. *I love you.*"

Andrew arched as lightning shot through his spine and spread like wildfire through his nervous system. He shouted as his orgasm hit him full force. He came all over the borrowed shirt.

"Oh," he muttered, panting.

His whole body shook in the aftermath of the strongest orgasm he'd ever experienced. If it was possible to go blind from an orgasm then Andrew needed to go and learn Braille. Andrew clawed at the arms wrapping around his waist.

"I love you too," he repeated in a broken whisper over and over until the shaking passed. The filters between his brain and his mouth had been completely torn down and he was talking nonsense.

When the aftershocks subsided and he got his breath back, Andrew was at a loss as to what to say. Blood rushed to his cheeks. There wasn't really much to say after he'd poured his heart out like a bad chick flick character and he wasn't in full enough control of his thoughts yet to come up with a plausible excuse.

He pulled away and rolled onto his side, facing Teddy.

"What just happened?"

Teddy just smiled back at him. A spark of heat should have clued Andrew in but being grabbed still made him squeak in surprise.

Suddenly he was on his back and Teddy was lying on top of him. He'd have been squished if his sexy fireman wasn't holding the majority of his weight on his big hands planted each side of Andrew's head.

He gulped. "Teddy?"

For a minute or two, all he could do was stare. At this angle, Teddy's arm bulged and the hem of the sleeves stretched so much Andrew detected the strain on the cotton stitches.

So hot.

The muscles twitched and contracted and Andrew couldn't look away. He darted his tongue out to wet his lips as he thought about tracing Teddy's bicep with it. Andrew snapped his eyes up when he realized Teddy was deliberately doing it.

Teddy was preening like a damn peacock.

"You seem to like my muscles. Perhaps I can hypnotize you and steal another kiss," Teddy joked. This time he made his pectorals dance. As much as Teddy joked, Andrew recognized the little hint of uncertainty in his expression.

A giggle tried to sneak past him. He slapped a hand up to cover his mouth. Andrew imagined Teddy was used to admiration and dazzling everyone but it didn't necessarily mean the man realized it.

Even when they were younger, before Teddy had the impressive bulk he now had, Andrew could literally stand behind him and watch people turn and ogle as Teddy walked by.

And they'd never had to pay at the movies for popcorn either. So they'd pretty much just lived off the stuff. Popcorn really should be considered a super food.

In his own head, Andrew was cool by association. In reality, it didn't make one damn bit of difference who he had as friends.

He was a geek. Always had been, always would be.

But that didn't mean a geek couldn't grope a fireman.

Watching Teddy's flexing display amazingly had Andrew's cock stirring again. Getting to run his hands all over Teddy was a dream come true. He reached to do just that when Teddy disappeared.

Okay, he didn't disappear but it seemed like it to Andrew's lust-addled mind.

To Andrew's relief, Teddy only pressed a kiss to his nose then got off the bed. Andrew tried to cover up, pulling at the sweats that were still below his ass and bearing his groin.

"Don't hide from me."

The command sizzled through him.

Andrew immediately dropped his hands to his sides. He swallowed nervously and shuddered as he waited for whatever was going to happen next. He liked Teddy telling him what to do a little too much.

"Take off the shirt, Drew," Teddy said huskily, eyes heavy-lidded.

At this point, his penis was at full attention and pointing directly toward Teddy like a dog awaiting its master's command. He knew he'd feel embarrassed later for giving in and so easily allowing Teddy to call the shots.

But right now? Right now, he was taking his damn shirt off.

Something told him Teddy knew the inner debate he was having when the man grinned and nodded. "Good boy," Teddy praised.

The 'boy' comment was a little too far and he managed to send Teddy a convincing glare but Teddy just looked at him with affectionate amusement.

"Your turn," Andrew snapped.

He almost swallowed his tongue when Teddy gripped the navy T-shirt and stripped it off, casting it aside to reveal the wide pecks and chiseled abs.

Holy crap.

There was perfect then there was godlike. Andrew didn't have to think long about which category to put Teddy in. Hell, he might even make a new one. Perfectly godlike.

He must have moved because Teddy gave him another teasing smile.

"Stay."

Another order. Another shudder of excitement.

Hyperventilating was definitely an option when Teddy reached for the button-fly of the khaki trousers. The fact that it was the station's uniform he was stripping out of made it even hotter.

The first button popped. Then the second. Then... Nothing.

Teddy stopped moving and Andrew's gaze flew from his lover's hands to his face. He knew this was too good to be true. Teddy must be having second thoughts. But did he have to be having them right now?

If Teddy turned around now and decided to skip back over to the heterosexual side of the fence, Andrew knew he was going to jump right over there with him and smack him with his own shoe.

But thankfully—and Andrew *was* damn thankful—Teddy only waited for Andrew's gaze to reach his eyes before giving another order.

"Take the sweats off."

Andrew swallowed hard and lifted his hips, keeping his gaze locked with Teddy's before pulling the sweats off. He waited for Teddy to say something more.

Teddy surprised him again by popping the final button of the trousers and letting them drop to the floor, along with his underwear.

Frozen, unable to look away from Teddy's sparkling baby blues, Andrew simply lay there. All he had to do was look down and he'd be able to see what Teddy looked like naked. He'd dreamed about it ever since he'd hit puberty.

And now that he was here, he couldn't make himself look down. He couldn't even blink.

After a few moments, he knew he was starting to look odd just lying there with his eyes wide and watering from lack of blinking.

Teddy cocked his head and lost the seductive expression.

Do something! His mind was literally in meltdown mode, but somehow he managed to force a smile that he prayed look somewhat normal. Judging by the concerned look Teddy offered him, he didn't succeed.

"You okay, Drew?"

Yeah, just dying of embarrassment of how not smooth he was. "I'm good." He nodded before trying a smirk and adding, "Just enjoying the view."

The forward comment paid off when Teddy turned a lovely shade of pink.

Ever so slowly, Andrew let his gaze fall. He traced the strong nose and jaw with his eyes. He let himself imagine being able to kiss the lips where the bottom one was just a little more plump, giving Teddy just the slightest bit of pout.

Andrew bet if he bit that lip, Teddy would look suitably debauched and the other firefighters would rib him good. Teddy would be marked and claimed. Not even Mr Dark Cloud would be able to dispute it.

He slid his attention lower and lingered on the smooth, defined chest. He froze again. This time it wasn't what he couldn't see that made him pause but what he *could* see.

A perfect tattoo of a teddy bear in a fireman's helmet with a heart as the emblem had been inked over Teddy's left pectoral. He'd forgotten about Steve mentioning it yesterday in the station's changing room.

He sat up and scooted to the edge of the bed for a better look. It was the same sketch he'd done years ago. Teddy had seen it by accident before Andrew could disguise it with other doodles and Andrew had quickly ripped out the page and thrown it away in an attempt to laugh it off.

The tattoo didn't look new either. Unsure whether he could touch it, he reached out but just left his hand out there, hanging.

Teddy didn't make him wait long. The man stepped forward, pressing his hand to the teddy-bear-inked chest. Andrew traced the lines in the Teddy's warm skin.

"When?" he asked.

"The first holiday you didn't come home. I needed something of you close to me," Teddy admitted, his voice rough and husky.

Andrew wasn't sure how to process having a family that loved him *and* a friend he'd been in love with possibly loving him back. It was all too much.

The panic-stricken claustrophobia rapidly returned.

Shaking his head to clear it, he found himself suddenly pressed into Teddy's stomach. It took precisely two seconds for him to remember that Teddy was naked.

He'd gone from being scared to touch Teddy to pushing his face into the man's rock-hard abs. *Naked,* rock-hard abs.

Naked. Naked. Naked.

The word kept spiraling around in his head, and he wasn't the only one not breathing.

An uncomfortable cough and a hand on the back of his neck broke the silence.

"Uh, Drew. I don't want to cheapen the moment but if you don't move your head this is going to be over really quick."

There was no way in hell he was able to stop his gaze from darting down when he pulled away. Holy moly. Teddy was huge—*huge!*

Like everything else about Teddy, the man's cock was a thing of beauty.

The shaft was at least nine inches and looked wide enough to split his lips if he tried to take the monster into his mouth. There was no way that was going to fit. *Anywhere.*

He must have said it aloud, because Teddy laughed.

"It'll fit. But we don't have to do anything you aren't comfortable doing. It's okay just being here with you."

There was his out.

Despite having mixed feelings about every other aspect of his life there was oddly nothing but certainty that Teddy would stop if he asked him to.

Which was ridiculous when he took into account he'd spent the last nine years hating the man.

Love songs didn't lie. Love really didn't make sense. It messed with his head until he wasn't sure he could tell his ass from his elbow.

"And if I want to try?" he asked, still looking at the erection in front of him.

Teddy placed his hand under Andrew's chin and lifted it so Andrew was looking him in the eyes again. It was another thing about Teddy that hadn't changed. The man believed in eye contact when he talked to someone.

"I'll let you do *anything*, Drew."

Now there was a sentence with a boatload of suggestion. Anything?

Andrew wasn't sure he was ready for what 'anything' referred to but that didn't mean he wouldn't remember it later. Right now, his mouth was watering and he had his sights set on something other than talking.

His focus must have flicked to where he wanted to taste, as the glint came back into Teddy's eyes, and Andrew caught a flash of perfect teeth. Teddy let him go and held his arms wide.

"I'm all yours, Drew. Ravish me," Teddy cried with a dramatic sigh.

He laughed at Teddy's antics and the ball of tension tangling in his stomach loosened. He didn't think he'd ever been this nervous. His previous encounters with men had been fast and usually ended in them calling him a tease because he wouldn't jump into bed with them.

Andrew figured he'd only live once. And this was definitely one of those once-in-a-lifetime opportunities that people talked about.

He took Teddy's cut penis in his hand, gripping the base firmly. He played his fingers over the velvety smooth surface and he liked the weight of Teddy's hot erection against his palm. The small, trimmed patch of hair surrounding it felt soft against his fist.

Science had always been his favorite subject but experiments had never been this fun. Every move he made solicited a reaction. When he squeezed, Teddy rocked up on his toes, and when Andrew pumped, Teddy thrust forward into Andrew's grip.

But what would Teddy do if he licked his big cock?

There was only one way to find out.

The second the tip of his tongue touched the bulbous head, Teddy made a sound somewhere between a moan and a squeal.

"Please, don't tease. I'm begging you," Teddy rasped.

Teddy gripped and loosened his hands repeatedly as though he didn't know what to do with them, so Andrew reached up and brought them to the top of his head to rest in his hair. He had no idea what had possessed him to do it but the moment Teddy's fingers tangled into Andrew's hair and tugged, Andrew was the one begging. The slight pain made him gasp and clench his ass cheeks.

That's intense.

"Again. Please pull my hair again," he asked desperately. His embarrassment filter must be offline. He wanted his hair pulled while he played with Teddy's cock. Looking at the big shaft made him want to taste it, so he licked his lips and pressed a kiss to the pink mushroom head then darted his tongue into the slit.

He kept his hand on the base and took Teddy's cock into his mouth. He could only fit the first few inches in without his gag reflex kicking in, urging him to cough. Hopefully moving one hand down to play with

Teddy's heavy balls while he pumped and squeezed his other would be enough to make up for his lack of technique and experience. Teddy seemed to enjoy whatever he did.

The salty taste grew stronger and Teddy's cries got louder.

A sharp tug on his hair made him groan and reach for Andrew's own erection.

His instinctive reaction was to gasp but with a mouth full of cock, all he could do was try not to choke. Without Andrew's hand holding the base of Teddy's dick, Teddy pushed deeper and touched the back of Andrew's throat for a second before pulling back.

Andrew's eyes watered at the feeling and his lips started to crack.

A twinge in his jaw told him he was about to get a killer cramp and he had to close his mouth as much as he could around Teddy to ward it off. Teddy took advantage of the tighter suction and thrust into his mouth. But Teddy never pushed past Andrew's limit.

The tight grip in his hair tugged again and Andrew knew he was about to lose control. A sharper yank would have hurt if not for the endorphins rushing through his system. But right now it was exactly what he needed and he groaned around Teddy's cock and came all over Teddy's leg.

If possible, Andrew could've sworn he'd stayed hard throughout the orgasm and continued to stand proud as he pleasured Teddy. Placing his hands on Teddy's powerful thighs, he patted the muscles until the man got the message and truly started fucking his mouth.

After two harder thrusts from Teddy, Andrew dug his fingers into thick thigh muscle and scraped his dull nails down them in angry red lines.

Teddy went off like a rocket. Burst after burst of hot release shot to the back of Andrew's throat. Andrew tried to swallow but it was just too much.

When the last eruption came from Teddy's spent cock, Andrew pulled back and turned away in a coughing fit. Somehow, Teddy had the presence of mind to bend him over so he had his head almost between his knees.

Then there were tissues cleaning off his face. The thought of what Teddy was wiping away penetrated his mind. Oh, crap. He'd really just given Teddy a blow job.

"Did you like it?" His insecurity struck and the question was out of his mouth before he could drag it back and bury it.

"It's pretty obvious that I liked it, Drew."

Teddy smiled when Andrew looked up at him before bending down and kissing the side of his mouth.

"But if you mean were you good," Teddy said, "then yes."

Another kiss, this time to the other side of Andrew's mouth.

"You were very, very good."

Andrew anticipated the kiss and moved to intercept it with his lips. A big part of him was still completely overwhelmed, but the rest of his body's desperation for Teddy to touch him drowned it out. If this was only going to happen once or if this was a dream then he wanted to feel as much as he could.

He chased Teddy's Cupid lips when and didn't duck out of the kiss until there was no air left in his lungs.

"Touch me?" He panted, grabbing on to Teddy's shoulders for support.

Teddy stood and Andrew had the split second decision to make whether to let go or cling on. He chose to cling on. Teddy didn't even pause at his weight, just slid arms under Andrew's ass and lifted him higher.

Teddy carried him to the middle of the bed. He laid Andrew on his back, lifting and spreading Andrew's legs before he even realized what Teddy was doing. Teddy immediately filled the space and Andrew shivered at just how wide he had to spread his legs to accommodate Teddy's impressive frame.

Teddy moved closer, leaning over him and pushing his legs back a little further. Andrew's ass was off the mattress now and the massive pole Teddy called a cock shoved right up against his balls and crevice.

"Oh." He gasped and clenched his cheeks around the hot erection.

"Are you sure you want to do this, Drew? I don't think I'm going to be able to give you up if you let me have you, if you let me love you," Teddy admitted, looking shaken but serious.

The words shocked him. A person didn't throw around words like the big L.

But that didn't surprise him as much as how serious Teddy looked. Staring up into the blue eyes Andrew had dreamed about for years, he couldn't help but believe the truth in them.

What could he say back to that?

He had no idea what was going to happen after his sister's wedding and his father's birthday. The original plan had been to run back to his cold, unfeeling life in the big city.

And go back to being alone and pretending that nothing touched him. Suddenly that plan didn't sound so good. But he couldn't see any other options. He still had to deal with his boss too and if he was honest, Andrew wasn't sure he realistically saw himself living here.

He'd been silent too long, and clearly Teddy had taken it as a rejection. "I don't want empty promises. I guess I just want you to give this—us—a shot. I'll move to the city, anything as long as I don't lose you again."

"I haven't made any decisions yet. But I want you. I've always wanted you. I need time to figure things out. C-c-can you give me that?" Here he was ready and aching to lose his virginity to his first love and he was risking blowing it all because he couldn't take a leap of faith.

Teddy nodded and gave him a small smile. "Yes, I can give you that."

Neither of them had softened as they'd talked, if anything the delayed pleasure and Teddy confessing he wanted more than a quick fuck made Andrew even harder. There was no way he was going to be able to come again but he didn't want this to end.

He wanted Teddy inside him.

Without another word, Teddy claimed his lips. He vaguely heard a soft click and squelch but he didn't think anything of it until something wet and cold rubbed around his clenching hole.

"It's just my finger. I need to get you ready."

Remembering the size of Teddy's erection made him question just how on earth he was ever going to be ready to take that.

He bit his lip to keep from moaning when the very tip of Teddy's finger breached his opening and

Andrew levered himself up to drag Teddy into another hungry kiss. "Hurry."

One finger changed to two when Teddy could comfortably get the first one in as far as it would go. Two fingers were nothing like just one. Teddy thrust them inside him and wiggled.

It felt odd but not bad so he sat up to watch. Since he was skinny and did a lot of running, he was flexible and could see Teddy pumping those thick fingers in and out of him.

When Teddy twisted his fingers inside him it was less pleasant but then he crooked them and hit something that made Andrew cry out and arch his back instinctively. His dick hit his stomach with a wet slap.

Holy Mother of God. Andrew may be a virgin but his computer was accustomed to porn. The prostate was a wonderful, wonderful thing with a skilled hand.

Teddy eased in a third finger and it burned a little more and made Andrew wince.

"Try to relax, baby," Teddy cooed in a ridiculous tone.

"Baby?" Drew he could put up with from Teddy and his family. But no way, no how was he answering to baby.

Nuh-uh.

Not happening.

Without stopping what he was doing with his fingers, Teddy grinned back at him with amusement. "Boo, pumpkin, honey, sugarplum, tickle bear, snookums?" Obviously the man had cracked and was having some sort of breakdown. But 'baby' didn't seem so bad now.

"Baby in a normal voice I can put up with but none of that cooing crap. I'm not a puppy," he said stubbornly. Secretly, he liked Teddy calling him by a pet name but the tone had to go.

"Baby," Teddy teased in that tone.

It distracted him enough that he'd been able to take Teddy's three fingers comfortably but the tentatively added forth almost had him crying uncle. Even with Teddy still hitting his button, it didn't take all of the pain away.

After another minute or two of stretching, the pressure eased as his muscles got used to Teddy's presence. "You're as stretched as I can make you, baby. Are you ready to try more?"

"Y-yes," he answered nervously.

This was really happening. He was about to have real, proper, sex-type sex. With *Teddy!*

The sound of a foil packet opening caught his attention and ramped up the nervous tension another notch.

Teddy picked up a tube Andrew hadn't noticed and squired a large blob of lube over that massive now-he-was-going-to-have-it-in-his-ass cock. He raised Andrew's legs so Andrew's calves rested over Teddy's wide shoulders.

"Tell me if it's too much and I swear I'll stop."

Giving him one last look, Teddy positioned the head of his cock at Andrew's entrance. Steadily the pressure increased. Andrew's ass burned and stretched far more than fingers had prepared him for.

He didn't like this bit at all.

Just when he thought he was really going to have to stop Teddy from going any further, the ring of muscle gave way to Teddy's insistent pushing. Slowly, Teddy sank into him.

"O-oh, so *full*." He panted. Holy hell.

With a couple of gentle thrusts, Teddy bottomed out. His lover was all the way inside him. The burning faded under the weight of the emotional rush. Teddy was *inside* him, a part of him with nothing between them but a thin wall of latex.

He'd love to feel Teddy inside him without anything between them but using protection was the smart thing to do. Andrew groaned and smacked his forehead when he realized he'd said it aloud.

"Maybe one day we can do that. If I can convince you to make a home with me," Teddy said with a panting laugh.

Andrew's leg muscles trembled and he thanked God he'd had a good run yesterday so they weren't likely to cramp up just yet. Even with the discomfort, this was the most intense thing he'd ever experienced.

The burn faded as Teddy stilled but Andrew could feel the slight trembles running through his body.

He blinked dreamily. Teddy watched him carefully. Teddy planted a hand on the bed either side of Andrew's head and leaned down to kiss him.

Damn, he was never going to get tired of kissing Teddy.

Teddy ghosted his lips down along Andrew's jaw and started sucking on Andrew's neck. The thought of Teddy marking him, claiming him, was magical. It certainly made the impossible happen as his balls tightened and pulled up against his body in warning of yet another impending orgasm.

"Don't come yet." The pleasure receded as Andrew obeyed Teddy's command.

"You ready for more?" Teddy asked.

Ready for more what? This was it, right? Sex equals penetration and that was it. Well unless he'd sat on a baseball bat, Teddy was as far inside him as he was going to get. There was no way the stuff he'd seen on porn was real.

Andrew nodded anyway, despite his reservations.

Teddy withdrew and slowly pushed back in. The outward stroke felt weird but the when his lover sank back into him it was awesome.

With his ass off the bed and legs over Teddy's shoulders, Andrew lay bent in just the right angle for Teddy to brush over the bundle of nerves inside him with every move.

"Oh, baby, *Drew!* Tell me to stop if I hurt you." Teddy grunted.

Before he could ask what Teddy meant, he found out. He nearly swallowed his tongue when Teddy withdrew and this time slammed back in to the hilt. "Ahh!"

Teddy's taut lower stomach smacked against him and every thrust was powerful enough to leave Andrew's cheeks stinging. He was getting spanked and skewered at the same time.

And it was un-fucking-believable.

When Teddy wrapped his hand around Andrew's pulsing erection, Andrew bucked but the position he was in only afforded him limited movement. It was just enough however to thrust against Teddy's hips.

Oh God, that felt good.

"Now!" Teddy's breathless demand instantly overloaded Andrew's system and he was helpless as he shot into orgasm again.

His ass locked down on Teddy's erection and he felt the spasm go through his lover. For a split second, it was as if time stood still and he dragged Teddy's face up from his neck so he could see his baby blues dilate.

So hot.

When the climax finally gave him mercy, he was spent, limp and gasping for breath. He could do nothing but lie there as Teddy collapsed to the side and hugged him close.

Teddy snuggled and spooned him from behind, disengaging their bodies as gently as possible. The movement still made Andrew wince, though. The mattress dipped as Teddy left the bed and he heard something land in the trash can.

It wasn't the most romantic sound when his world was still spinning on someone else's axis. But he forgot all about it when Teddy got back into bed and curled around him.

Somehow, he managed to reach back and to bring Teddy's arm around his waist, cuddling it close so the man was draped over him like his own personal blanket.

Teddy's lips tickled Andrew's skin as Teddy pressed a kiss to Andrew's neck and gave a contented sigh. "Give me ten minutes and we can go for round four in the shower?"

Round four?

In the shower?

Andrew wasn't going to survive.

Chapter Ten

One minute he was in a lovely dream where he lived in a warm house with Teddy, a cat and a few dogs and Teddy had just come home from work still in his uniform, next, someone kept shaking him awake.

Dream Teddy was just starting to sway to music and reach for the bright red suspenders when the image was ripped away.

"No! It was just getting good. He even had the uniform," he cried in grief as he tried to get the dream back.

"Uniform?"

The question woke him up a little more until he opened his eyes to see Teddy, dressed in shorts looking at him in confusion.

"Uh, never mind. What's up?"

"Up and at 'em, Drew. We need to leave." Teddy spoke quickly, pulling him to his feet and stuffing his arms into T-shirt sleeves and handing him sweats.

"I cannot catch a break." He sighed then yawned deeply.

"The fire alarm hasn't gone off but I know the sounds of a fire eating up a house. We need to get out now. I didn't smell the smoke until I got to the back of the house so it's still early."

Andrew found himself dragged out of the bedroom before he even understood the words. Adrenaline shot through him when he registered what Teddy had said. Fire? As in the house they were currently in was on fire?

Suddenly he was wide-awake and terrified as he gripped Teddy's hand tighter and let Teddy pull him down the hall. The stairs were in the other direction but before he could ask, Teddy opened a door on the left and he saw a smaller set of stairs.

It was very dark and darkened further to almost pitch black when Teddy pushed them in and closed the door behind them.

"This used to be the servants' staircase. We can't turn the light on since I don't know whether it's an electrical fire or not. Don't let go of my hand." Teddy carefully but quickly led them down the stairs.

When they reached the bottom, Andrew smelled the thick, choking smoke leaking from under the door.

"Shit! The fire is either spreading with an accelerant or there was more than one point of origin." Teddy swore quietly.

Suddenly there were hands pulling at his clothes. "Put your shirt over your head and don't take deep breaths." When he'd done as ordered Teddy lifted him up without so much as a grunt and placed him in a fireman's carry, draped across the back of Teddy's big shoulders.

Teddy moved one of his legs over his arm so he could come through Andrew's legs and lock over his other knee, holding Andrew securely. One of

Andrew's arms was tugged over Teddy's other shoulder to keep him steady as he held the shirt to his face with the other.

Andrew's heart pumped hard and fast at this point. How serious was this? Teddy was calm so it couldn't be that bad. Unless Teddy was calm *because* it was that bad. Without being able to see the expression on his lover's face, all Andrew could do was guess.

"Close your eyes, tuck your head and don't look up."

The second the last word left Teddy's lips Andrew heard a door being kicked open.

"Oh, fuck," he cursed and winced, shrinking into Teddy.

They'd only gone a few feet when the heat hit Andrew. It was like standing in the middle of a sauna. And the smoke was bleeding through the fabric of his shirt.

He knew he shouldn't. Teddy had explicitly said not to but he just had to look. When he opened his eyes, he could see through the thin fabric of the shirt.

And immediately wished he hadn't.

Angry red and orange walls closed in around them as Teddy twisted and turned through the house.

Oh shit. Oh shit. Oh shit.

Andrew dug his head back down into Teddy's shoulder and closed his eyes against the sting of the thick, black smoke but he could hear the roaring now. Bangs and groans came from behind them and he flinched at every one.

Something hit his back with burning sharpness and he cried out in pain. "Fuck!"

He knew Teddy was speaking to him but he couldn't make out the words. Andrew just wanted to get out of there.

Teddy tensed his arm, tightening his hold on him. Andrew had just enough time to brace himself before there was a mighty crash. A thunderous roar followed it then he was on the ground being rolled and covered by Teddy.

Someone pulled his shirt off then he came face-to-face with his lover.

Teddy's lips moved but he couldn't process what he was saying.

Giving up, Teddy resorted to hand gestures and Andrew realized he needed to get up and move. When they were about thirty feet from the house, he noticed Teddy was holding something.

His backpack.

On the way out of the burning house, Teddy must have grabbed his bag. In it were Andrew's laptop, phone and the photos of him and Teddy he'd taken from his old room at his parents' house that his mother had given him after they'd gone to the hotel. Teddy could have left the bag or better yet saved something of his own but instead had chosen to rescue Andrew's backpack.

The smoke already had his eyes watering but the now the tears weren't just a physical reaction.

Teddy raised the bag and started riffling through it until he found Andrew's phone. He watched as Teddy held it out to him but didn't take it.

What did Teddy want him to do—oh!

Snatching the phone, he quickly entered the password to enable a new user and handed it back.

He turned away as Teddy rang the station and watched the house burn. A smash drew his attention to the second floor. The windows had exploded. Flames engulfed the ground and first floors.

Even from here, he could feel the heat reaching for them.

Teddy wrapped his arms around Andrew and they moved farther back until the heat only glowed at them. All the work Teddy had put into that house was gone. And all Andrew could do was turn and hug his lover tightly.

They stood like that until he heard the sirens.

* * * *

The fire engines got there in time to save the structure of the house but everything inside was toasted. The nice fellow he'd met at the fire station had come straight over to make sure they were okay before diving in with the other firefighters to battle the blaze.

Apparently the fire chief had called a crew of paramedics and Andrew was currently sitting in an ambulance being checked over as Teddy tried to get some information out of the other firefighters.

Andrew spotted Teddy standing closer to the fire with a man someone had pointed out before as the fire chief. Teddy talked animatedly and shook his head at something the chief said. Teddy gestured to the house then over to him. The older man spoke again and grabbed Teddy's arm as Teddy went to move away. Andrew couldn't hear what they were saying but it was obviously a tense conversation.

Teddy looked his way and met his gaze but there was none of the happy, easy-going personality there. Which was understandable since the man's home had just burned down. Well not down, since it was still standing but everything inside looked black through the burned-out window frames.

He tried to smile reassuringly but the paramedic chose that exact moment to probe the wound on his back. Most likely he had some glass in it or something else but did the woman really need to push her finger in to find out?

He might not have kept up his emergency medic training but he was sure it hadn't changed to include stabbing patient's wounds.

"Is that necessary?"

"There's something imbedded in the wound. I need to see what it is before I can treat it. So sit still and put up with it," the paramedic answered sharply before continuing the torture.

"It's probably wood or glass from things exploding in the fire," he snarled through gritted teeth. Sitting on the step of an ambulance wasn't the most comfortable position but at least here, he could see what was going on. He'd refuse to sit on the stretcher in case they tried to take him off to hospital.

A grunt was the only answer he got then the paramedic froze and jumped to her feet. She left him sitting there as she ran over to Teddy and the fire chief.

"No its fine, go ahead and leave. It not like I'm bleeding or in pain or anything," he called sarcastically.

The other paramedic snorted as he sat there listening to his heart but simply continued what he was doing. He then shoved a breath analyzer in his face. "Breathe into this, it will test how much smoke you inhaled."

She came back with Teddy and the fire chief hot on her heels. Teddy looked almost panicked, which immediately put Andrew on edge, and he reached out for his lover. He placed the breath tester aside.

"What's going on? Are you okay, Teddy?"

Teddy let out a laugh that sounded more like a cry and dropped to his knees in front of him. With the height difference and Andrew sitting on the step it put them at eye level. "Am I okay?" The crack in Teddy's voice might have been from smoke inhalation but Andrew wasn't sure.

"You're scaring me." Andrew tried to reach out and get Teddy to sit up in the ambulance with him but his paramedics slash interrogators *tsked* and stopped him moving.

"I'm fine, baby. How are you? Is the pain manageable? I can get Catherine to give you a sedative if it's too bad," Teddy gushed. He passed his big hands over Andrew's body as if checking for more injuries.

"I'm okay, Teddy. Apart from the cut on my back that's starting to hurt like a bitch, I'm fine. Just a few scratches," he replied, catching Teddy's hands in his own.

"He's in shock and the bullet didn't hit straight on so much as graze him and lodge itself in the flesh just under the latissimus dorsi muscle," the female paramedic — Catherine — explained.

"Huh?" The fire chief gave him a look of suspicion before turning back to the paramedic.

"He was shot, Burt!" Teddy shouted at the fire chief.

"And he's fine. Stand down, Goldbloom," the chief retorted, sounding exasperated and confused as to why Teddy was so freaked out.

Andrew had the distinct feeling he was missing something important to the conversation.

Wait a minute.

"Shot?" Andrew's breathing started to get shorter and shallower as he looked at Teddy and the whole of the conversation finally sank in.

"He was shot in the back of the ribs," Catherine answered the older man with an eye roll. She continued to ignore him, though, which just served to piss Andrew off.

"Uhm, not be rude or anything but can we focus on the fact that someone *shot* me!" When he thought it was just a piece of glass digging into him, it hadn't hurt too much. Now that he knew it was a fucking bullet, he was on the verge of passing out.

Catherine stepped back up into the van.

He heard some plastic packets opening. Then something stabbed him. "Ow!"

He tried to pull away but hands on his shoulders kept him still and numbness started spreading over his back.

"Better?" she asked.

"Yeah, thanks," he mumbled. Shouldn't people be as freaked out as he was about the fact that he'd been shot?

A pressure on his back let him know she was prodding him again but the pain was gone. Teddy caught his attention by squeezing his hand and Andrew realized he'd been asked a question.

"Sorry can you repeat that, please?"

The fire chief stepped into his line of vision and glared down at him as if he was a misbehaving child. "Do you know anyone who'd want to shoot you, Mr Finley?"

"Absolutely not!" Andrew scowled at the man, insulted by the insinuation that he was a troublemaker, even though he could come up with a handful of people right off the bat. He stubbornly tried not to think about the name written in his mind with big flashing lights.

Consciously trying not to reveal his deception, he made a show of smoothing back his hair so his hand covered his face. The man already disliked him so a display of flamboyance wouldn't make much difference.

Sure enough, the old guy's gray brows furrowed and he curled his lip.

Andrew had to concentrate on not looking at Teddy when he sensed the chief's gaze on him, searching.

Teddy came to his defense and tackled his boss's accusing looks and questions head on. "Who would want to shoot him, Chief? He's only been back a day or two."

"Just take the bullet out, please, Catherine." Andrew sighed, diverting attention away from the questions he could almost feel Teddy thinking at him, despite jumping to his defense.

Realistically, Andrew knew he should go to hospital to have the bullet removed but he couldn't afford those few hours right now. Whoever had shot him wasn't likely to be here now with the place crawling with police and firefighters but that didn't mean the perpetrator wasn't close by or waiting for another shot.

"You need to go to hospital for that," she replied.

"You either take it out here or it will just have to stay there." He was eighty percent sure her paramedic training would kick in and she wouldn't let him really walk off with a bullet lodged inside him.

Andrew needed a place to lie low and think. But most of all he wanted to get Teddy the hell out of there. The last thing he wanted was for Teddy to become a target for some nutcase taking shots and setting fires.

The shock must have addled his brain. It just then sank in that it was his fault that Teddy's house and all his belongings were crispy.

"Oh, fuck," he cursed. He played it off as pain when everyone looked at him but the crushing sense of guilt threatened to swallow him whole.

Teddy had lost everything because of him.

* * * *

The fire chief had eventually gotten bored of questioning him and the firefighters had gotten the blaze down to a simple smolder. It had been hours since the ambulance had turned up and the painkiller Catherine had given him had long since worn off.

But at least he could see properly now having found a spare set of glasses in his bag.

"You need to take some painkillers," Teddy repeated for the third time in the last five minutes.

Since Andrew knew Teddy realized he was keeping secrets, his wound had been one of the only things they'd talked about.

Teddy had told him what the fire chief had concluded about the fire. Accelerants had been used in three separate areas, all of them exits.

When he'd gotten his phone back and snuck out from under the hawk-like gaze of Catherine the Poker for some privacy, he'd called Agent Christopher Hammer and the man had said he'd be there as soon as he could. That had been an hour ago.

The last of the crews packed up and the truck drove off. Every crew member had offered them a bed for the night or to drive them somewhere but he'd managed to convince everyone that his sisters were coming soon. Luckily, Steve wasn't on duty. Andrew knew he was going to pay for that lie later but right now, he had little choice. He was just thankful Teddy had gone along with it.

Now they were alone, sitting in Teddy's truck until Christopher turned up. Hairs on the back of Andrew's neck stood up as he thought of someone possibly spotting him through their crosshairs.

"Can you slouch a bit, please?" Blacked-out windows would help hide them but it wouldn't stop a bullet.

Teddy didn't look entirely shocked at his request but didn't move to comply either. His lover just sat there looking at Andrew with a mix of anger and concern. "Are you going to tell me what's going on?"

"Yes, I swear I'll tell you everything, just *please* scoot down as far as you can," he insisted, trying to pull Teddy over in the seat.

Teddy seemed to think about it for a minute and Andrew kept trying to tug him down. Coming to some sort of decision, Teddy did as he requested.

As soon as both of them were as scrunched up as low in their seats as possible, Teddy shook off his hands and looked him dead in the eye. "Talk."

Andrew tried not to let it show how hurt he was that Teddy wouldn't let Andrew touch him. Andrew quickly looked away when Teddy continued to stare at him. He took a deep breath to calm his nerves.

After all the revelations about the past, was his present going to be the thing that ended his chance of something real with Teddy?

"Hey," Teddy whispered.

He settled a big hand settled on Andrew's knee and squeezed lightly.

He turned back to see Teddy still hunched over but his expression had softened. It was a start.

"Just tell me, okay? I don't like being in the dark. Especially after the last time there were secrets between us."

Nodding, Andrew placed his hand over Teddy's and let out a sigh of relief when his lover turned it over and laced their fingers together. When had he become so needy?

"I don't work for a tech support company. In short, I was naughty in college and hacked a few places I shouldn't have and I was given an ultimatum by the CIA—work for them or go to prison. My boss is up to something shady, has been for a while, and knows I'm looking for a way to stop him. Genie went out with a guy who's helping me use the information I have. And I'm ninety-nine percent certain my employer is the person who shot me and I'm so so *so* sorry he set fire to your house." By the time he'd finished he was out of breath and had to shove his glasses back up on his nose since they'd almost fallen off when he was talking animatedly.

Teddy just stared at him for a moment then spared a snort of disbelief. "That was the short version?"

He was still heaving in a breath, wincing when it aggravated his injury, so he just nodded again. At this rate, he was going to turn into one of those dashboard toys.

"So this guy is after you because he's done something wrong and you have proof that will hold him accountable? Just yes or no please otherwise my head is likely to implode," Teddy asked when Andrew opened his mouth to explain.

"Yes," Andrew answered obediently.

"And he tried to kill you by setting my house on fire and shooting you as well?"

"Yes," he repeated as his guilt doubled.

"And this Agent Hammer is coming here now?"

"Yes."

"Are you in pain?"

"Yes." *More like hell yes.* His back felt like the bullet had been made of freaking acid and had burned a hole all the way down to his damn soul. Andrew really didn't have a high pain threshold.

"Are you staying with me?" Teddy changed the line of questioning.

"Yes." Where else would he be?

"Do you love me?"

"I... Yes." It was different to admit it when he wasn't overwhelmed by pleasure while they were making love but Andrew forced himself to be honest.

All sense of anxiousness from Teddy was gone, replaced by a smug grin and the spark was back in the blue eyes. Andrew thought perhaps it was time for a little turnabout to clear up a few things.

"My turn?"

Teddy nodded and gestured for him to take the floor so to speak.

"Go ahead. I like this," Teddy said confidently.

"We'll see if you feel the same way after a few questions," he scoffed. There was one question he really needed an answer to.

"Were you ever engaged to Angela?" Biting his lip, he waited.

"What! No!"

Good to know. There wasn't any hint of a lie and Teddy hadn't been anything other than honest since Andrew had come back. Andrew even cracked a bit of a smile at the distaste Teddy managed to get into the two words.

"Did you ever sleep with Angela? Wait! Don't answer that one, I don't want to know," he rushed to contradict himself. Angela was a slut so of course Teddy had slept with her.

"Not after you turned fifteen," Teddy answered quietly, sounding ashamed.

"Really?" That wasn't long before he'd left.

"Yes. I'm four years older than you are. I liked you but there was no way I could ask you out until you were at least eighteen because of the age difference. Then you were gone."

That was a shock.

"Do you believe me? You know, about working for the CIA and my boss trying to kill me?" Andrew wouldn't blame him if he didn't. It was a lot for a person to take on faith.

"It's hard not to when you've been shot and my house is crispy. Yes."

Now there was only one question left needed to ask.

"Do you love me?" Andrew asked.

"Yes."

"You know that's the only question you answered properly," he said with a smirk as his phone buzzed with a text alert.

"Yes." Teddy winked.

Laughing, he flinched again but couldn't help the relief that Teddy still wanted him. He checked his cell and saw Agent Hammer was close by just as he heard the hum of an approaching car.

Teddy heard it too as the man tensed and looked ready to either dive over him to be a human shield or leap out of the truck and face the threat barehanded. As if carrying him out of a burning building and saving his computer and photos hadn't made him heroic enough.

Andrew thought he might swoon.

He squeezed Teddy's hand to reassure him. "It's Agent Hammer."

Teddy nodded but didn't look any more relaxed.

A black car with dark windows and out-of-state plates pulled up next to them on Andrew's side. His phone beeped again. The message said to stay in the car until Christopher knocked on the window.

Teddy hadn't moved his position and was looking at something over Andrew's head, so Andrew guessed Teddy could see what Agent Hammer was doing.

"There's another guy with him and they're doing a perimeter check by the looks of it with strange binoculars. Infrared goggles maybe?"

"Cool." Andrew had always wanted to take a closer look at a kit like that. Maybe he could manufacture his own scanner and incorporate it into his phone somehow. He fiddled with his glasses as he started plotting out the device he had in mind.

"Yes, I suppose if you think searching for a rogue CIA agent who wants to kill you is cool," Teddy responded with an expression that clearly stated he was humoring Andrew.

Before he could think of any kind of comeback, someone knocked on his window. "It's all clear, Mr Finley. We need you to get in the car right now." He didn't recognize the voice so it must have been the other man Teddy had said was there.

Andrew looked at Teddy to see what his reaction was but Teddy kept his face calm, hiding whatever he was thinking.

"Andrew we need to go *now*." This time it was Agent Hammer who rapped on the window and called to him.

"Coming!" He gave one last look at Teddy and sighed in relief when Teddy gave a nod and motioned for him to get out of the truck. If Teddy needed to be in charge that was fine with Andrew—as long as Teddy was here.

The second his feet touched the ground, as he gingerly slid out of the truck, the man that wasn't Agent Hammer grabbed him by the shoulders and yanked him over to the car.

He couldn't hold in the cry of pain as his wound throbbed under the pressure of being bent over and shoved into a car.

"Ow! Shit," he cursed as agony rippled through him.

He cursed again at the rush of searing heat as his back hit the car seat. He was sure he blacked out for a second. The sound of shouting and the scuffs of shoes grinding on the gravelly dirt forced him to look back out the door.

"What the hell do you think you're doing? Unhand me!" Thurgood hollered.

"Sir, let go of Agent Thurgood," Agent Hammer interjected.

He glanced to the left and saw Teddy holding Agent Thurgood by the throat up against the blue truck.

"Teddy! P-put him down," he shouted as he tried to shake off a wave of dizziness. The thought that Christopher was going to hurt his lover if he didn't do something urged him to move so that he was hanging out of the car. It hurt like a bitch but if he put his hand on the seat in front of him, he could keep most of the pressure off.

Teddy looked at him but continued to ignore the struggles and orders from the agents. "Not until he apologizes. He could have seriously hurt you. Catherine said that if you stressed the wound too much it could cause internal bleeding," Teddy answered, still not releasing the grip on the agent's shirt collar.

Agent Hammer stopped pulling at Teddy since he really wasn't having any impact but he didn't let go. "Agent Thurgood, just apologize so we can move to a more secure location!"

"I am not apologizing for doing my job!" Agent Thurgood's words were barely legible as the man struggled and started to turn a shade of purple.

Andrew sat forward slowly, finally easing away from the seat behind him. The fabric of his shirt stuck to his skin, letting him know he'd started bleeding again. But he didn't say anything. It would only ignite things further. It didn't feel like a lot of blood. If that changed then he'd say something.

"You were rough and you know it. I'm pulling rank, now apologize," Agent Hammer said, releasing Teddy and pointing at the man in question.

"Fine. I apologize for any behavior you may have considered more forceful than necessary," Thurgood ground out. It was anything but sincere but it seemed enough to appease Teddy. He dropped the man then came over to Andrew.

Teddy gently scooted him over in the seat and got in next to him before closing the door. They both watched the men outside the car.

Hammer and Thurgood huddled together, whispering, and whatever was said seemed to put Thurgood in his place. Teddy took Andrew's hand and gave it a squeeze. Andrew couldn't put into words how grateful he was that Teddy hadn't run screaming for the hills. So he just settled for, "Thank you."

Teddy was taking everything extremely well. Disturbingly well, actually.

Narrowing his eyes at his lover, Andrew tried to ignore Agents Thurgood and Hammer getting into the front of the car. The awkwardness ramped up.

"Why *are* you taking this so well?" Andrew asked Teddy

"Firefighters don't freak out until the fire is under control and we're home safe. Even though my house is only smoldering, we're not out of the fire yet." Teddy gave a meaningful look at the two men in the front seats before leaning over to him. "And I don't trust whoever these people are either," he said in a quiet voice.

It wasn't the response he'd been expecting. But it wasn't one he could argue with either. Andrew turned more into the warmth of Teddy's much bigger body. Teddy immediately slung his arm around Andrew's shoulders and let him cuddle into his side.

Andrew tensed as Teddy moved the arm he had around Andrew's shoulders and started combing fingers through his hair. He relaxed into the touch. It was nice and it took Andrew's mind off the pain.

"How many people knew you were staying with me?"

He frowned as he thought of what Teddy was saying—or rather not saying. And he started compiling a mental list. He really didn't think Genie, Sara or Steve would sell him out and that only left Agent Hammer.

Then a thought struck him—the receptionist. Teddy had helped him pack up his stuff and she had been in the background messing with her phone.

"The receptionist?" he voiced his thought.

Teddy's mouth contracted into a thin line. "She's a good friend of Angela's. But do you really think your sister is capable of this?"

"She got the football team to attack me, assault me and scar me while she kidnapped you from your sick bed, possibly drugged you, all to run me out of town so she could get you to marry her. She's also drugged at least one man to ruin his marriage." The list wasn't pleasant. And stated aloud, it was shocking to know they shared the same blood.

Teddy did an impression of an owl, wide-eyed and speechless.

"Sorry. Hearing you try and defend her kind of pissed me off," he said through clenched teeth as he tried to move away. With his throat tightening up with tension, anger and smoke inhalation, it hurt like a bitch to even force the words out, but not as much as hearing Teddy jump up to sing Angela's praises.

His lover was immediately contrite and apologetic. "I'm sorry! I don't know why I tried to defend her." Teddy's face screwed up in a wince.

Andrew let Teddy tilt his head up and pressed soft kisses to his lips. "I'm sorry. I love you, Drew. Don't pull away because I'm an idiot."

Okay, he was a pushover. But he never got used to hearing Teddy say those words to him.

"Just try to remember she's not the innocent little girl she tried to make you think she was," he warned, unwilling to let the subject drop completely. Angela was dangerous.

"Not to interrupt this late-night special but are you saying Angela Finley—your *sister*—is the one you think who sold you out to our suspect?" The disgust and disbelief in Thurgood's voice let him know the man was either an only child or one of those rare people who came from a functional family.

"She's the only one who would want me dead as much as Martin does. So if he's looking for information as to where I am then it makes sense he'd look up my family. It doesn't take a competent CIA agent to discover the bad blood between Angela and me," he muttered tiredly, rubbing the arm of his glasses.

When were people going to take him at his word when he said she was evil? It would save a hell of a lot of time.

He dreaded to think what his mother was going to say when he came clean about what he did and that his boss had teamed up with his sister to try to kill him. It had the makings of a cheesy TV show. It was a conversation he was not looking forward to.

Thinking about how far Angela might go to get back at him for stealing Teddy from her made him pause. "I need you to put some of your people, whoever the hell you work for, on my family in case Angela goes even further into this craziness. Martin isn't above using family as leverage either."

He sensed Teddy's gaze on him as he went on to talk with Agent Hammer about the evidence he'd gathered and his suspicions but he didn't look up. The sooner he got his mess sorted out, the sooner he could start making it up to Teddy for sticking with him. He didn't think many people would take everything in stride like this. Andrew was a bag of nerves.

"I have to say, Andrew, the evidence is solid. All the information has checked out so far and has even brought to light a few more names we need to look into as well. After all this, you might want to consider coming to work for us," Agent Hammer offered.

Andrew wasn't expecting the job offer, even after the man had hinted at it during their meeting with Genie. He couldn't think about anything like that yet. And he had the distinct feeling that he wouldn't be making the decision alone. "I need to talk it over with my boyfriend. But thank you for the offer. I'll give it some thought," he answered without giving an affirmation or a rejection.

It was enough for Christopher. They sat the rest of the way in relative silence. Andrew didn't have to look up to know Teddy was grinning and feeling pleased. When they were younger, Teddy had always liked when Andrew included him in decisions and he doubted that had changed.

"I'm your boyfriend, huh? Does that mean you're going to move in? You know, when the house stops smoking," Teddy amended with a shrug. Teddy's sandy-colored hair was almost black from the fire and he had black smudges all over his face, making Teddy look like he'd just jumped out of a fireman calendar.

But it was his grin that made Andrew shake his head in exasperation. Teddy was smug and smiling like a Cheshire cat. He could see that Teddy knew what his answer was going to be before he did.

"Well I don't know..." he tried to hedge unconvincingly. It would serve Teddy right if he said no.

"You will. We'll have to draw you a computer gadget room in the new house plans. It might take a while for us to get past a bedroom and kitchen, though. I've been doing the place up as I could afford it." His happiness diminished as the sentence continued and Teddy began to look worried.

"I have money," Andrew pointed out helpfully but that only made Teddy frown harder. "This is going to turn into a macho thing, isn't it?"

Andrew groaned and wondered if there was one of those *For Dummies* books about relationships, because going by how tactful his last comment was, he was going to need it. He overlooked the slight panic at the thought he might actually be in a relationship. There was only enough room in his head to panic about one thing at a time.

Chapter Eleven

They'd set up base above the fire station after Teddy had pulled in a favor from the building owner. It had been decided that the only way to catch Martin was to either find Angela or draw Martin out.

Teddy was all for plan A and refused to even discuss plan B but Andrew had been in this business long enough to know plan A never worked. As a rule of thumb, plan D or E ended up being the final play.

Agent Christopher Hammer had assured him that his other sisters were fine as well as his parents and that all were protected. Andrew had phoned them to make sure and his mother had demanded to speak to 'whoever the heck was in charge of her little boy's safety'.

Agent Hammer had wisely passed that honor on to Agent Thurgood and the man looked as if he had been ripped a new one, which had been amusing as hell to watch. At least until his father had come on the line to grill him about what he actually did for a living. For the life of Andrew, he couldn't remember why on earth he'd wanted his parents to take an active interest in his life or talk to him more. Teddy had even had a turn talking to his parents and whatever was said turned his lover bright red and had him promising something but Teddy wouldn't spill the beans.

Agent Hammer had quizzed his sisters and parents on speakerphone about where Angela would go if she needed to hide then dispatched people there to check them out.

So far, they hadn't had any luck.

Agent Hammer's people were on the last location now. Apparently, Angela still slept with and manipulated the ex-captain of the football team, despite the man having a wife and two kids.

The man kept an apartment in town for her, all bills covered. The slut business paid well it seemed. And the deeper Andrew delved into her financials the more shit he found. There were at least six men paying into her account every month or so, in equal amounts that just screamed blackmail payments.

Scrolling down the page on his computer, Andrew stopped at two payments made by the same person a week apart and both were substantially higher than any other payments into the account.

But that wasn't all that caught Andrew's attention. "I found something."

Agent Hammer and Teddy stopped talking about places Martin could go to lay low and walked over to him.

"What is it, baby?"

Andrew ignored the snort from Agent Thurgood and pointed at the screen, highlighting the two payments he'd found. "See the account number there? That's the same number as one of the accounts I put in my notes that I thought belonged to Martin."

"So?"

"So one of them is from before Drew came back home," Teddy pointed out with a look of distrust aimed at Thurgood.

Not bothering to hide his smile, Andrew blew Teddy a kiss before turning to Agent Hammer. "This means Martin was probably planning on me coming home for him to kill me all along."

"We can use it, right?" Teddy asked him, leaning down to take a closer look at the screen.

"Yep. I can't track her phone since she dumped her old one but Angela was always the type to look at her money so she probably has a phone app for her bank account. And if Martin has been making transfers to her then he'll have a similar app too," he explained as he initiated the tracking program.

It should take less than ten minutes to track down their phones and their locations. People thought they were smart getting new phones and dumping old ones when they went on the run but that didn't always mean a person was untraceable.

"And?" Thurgood wasn't stupid but he didn't come across as much of a tech person either.

"And that means I can find them, Agent Thurgood, as well as prove the transfers, accounts and phones are theirs." The program was already at forty percent. As soon as it was completed, Andrew would have them.

Thurgood and Hammer shared a look then wandered off as the crackle of a radio signaled the last team had checked in.

Teddy stayed with Andrew and glanced between him and the laptop as if he was seeing him for the first time. "You really like this stuff, don't you? All this computer tracking," he said gesturing to the equipment. "It's like you light up."

"I'm good at it and... I don't know. It's just my thing," Andrew answered, shrugging.

Teddy nodded thoughtfully then flashed him a smile that was all white teeth and animalistic intent. "I wonder if I could make you light up like that?"

Andrew didn't reply. But he didn't have to. They both knew Teddy lit him up like the Fourth of July. Hell, he was hard now, despite his back still aching like a sore tooth and Agents Thurgood and Hammer standing only ten feet away from them.

He slapped at Teddy's hand as his lover reached out to fiddle with one of the wires. "Be good."

"I'm always good with you," Teddy teased back, stroking over Andrew's shoulders in a light massage.

Since they'd been there, Teddy had switched back and forth between light teasing and serious support, giving Andrew exactly what he needed, when he needed it. He tilted his head back so their faces were only an inch apart.

"Your program is done," Teddy said against his lips.

He tried to look at his laptop but something obscured the screen. Then he realized it was his glasses. The lenses had actually steamed up. "Damn things." He ripped them off his face and scrunched the bottom of his T-shirt to wipe them clean, pointedly not looking at Teddy as the man guffawed.

He inspected the glasses and wiped them again. A knock sounded at the door and Teddy hopped up from where he'd been perched next to him on the desk. "I'll get it. It's probably one of the guys bringing up the food."

Putting his glasses back on, Andrew looked back at the screen and nearly fell out of the chair. Jumping to his feet, he ignored the pain and ran after Teddy. He all but tackled Teddy and motioned frantically at the door as the agents looked at him like he'd lost his mind.

Still hanging on Teddy's back, he whispered, "They're here!"

Teddy froze, letting Andrew slide down his body, then pressed Andrew against his back, hiding him effectively. Agents Thurgood and Hammer unsheathed their weapons and took up positions on either side of the door. Thurgood opened the door.

Teddy backed them up so they were further away from the entrance.

He held his breath as Thurgood turned the lock and swung the door open. It was like a car crash. No matter how much Andrew didn't want to see, he couldn't make himself look away.

"How did they know we were here?" Teddy asked.

Only the people in this room and a few firefighters who'd seen them come up knew they were there. But if he had to guess then Thurgood was a likely option. There was nothing they could do about it at the moment anyway.

The door swung open. It took Andrew a second or two to recognize the face. The Mr Dark Cloud firefighter who'd refused to tell him where Steve was. *Glowering must be the guy's superpower.*

But no Martin. And no Angela.

The agents checked behind the man and stood down, waving the firefighter inside. Teddy moved too, leaving Andrew wishing the ground would swallow him up. Something must have gone wrong with the program.

Mr Dark Cloud put the bags of food on the table.

Thurgood shot him a look of disgust when Andrew tried to edge around everyone and head back to his laptop. He couldn't understand what had gone wrong.

Teddy turned and caught his hands as he passed and squeezed them to get his attention. "Hey. We'll just try again. No biggie," Teddy comforted softly.

Andrew nodded and tried to smile but he was too embarrassed.

Agents Thurgood and Hammer closed the door behind Mr Dark Cloud and came over to the table to dig through the bags of food.

Perhaps he'd made a mistake in the programming sequence but he ran the numbers in his head and they all seemed fine.

He set the program to run again and joined everyone else at the table. He put his hand into the closest bag and pulled out a bag of chips. He reached back in to see what else was in there and felt something strange, something small and heavy.

Grabbing it, he pulled it out. What the hell?

It was a phone. Or rather, two phones taped together.

A beep behind him announced the program had run again. Andrew didn't have time to speak before all hell broke loose. Mr Dark Cloud stepped back from the table with a smirk a split second before the door burst open and someone started shooting.

Instinct made Andrew duck down but he spun around and searched for Teddy. He couldn't see him anywhere. "Teddy!"

Andrew crawled on his hands and knees, moving in a circle as he tried to see all the room. He saw agents Thurgood and Hammer with their weapons up again and shooting back.

Bits of brick and plasterboard flew everywhere as bullets gouged holes in the walls. His ears were ringing with the constant abuse from gunshots but he could hear them getting closer to him as he crawled.

He spotted Teddy just as Teddy punched out Mr Dark Cloud. The man dropped like a stone, collapsing into a heap. Teddy spun around looking for something then spotted Andrew on the floor and ran toward him. To Andrew's relief, Teddy ducked as another rain of bullets tore through the room.

A big chunk flew right over Andrew's head. He flinched but kept moving. He needed to get to Teddy. There wasn't much to hear apart from the gunfire and shouting but he hoped Agent Hammer had managed to radio for backup because Martin was pretty much kicking their asses.

While the Agents had handguns, Martin had some sort of automatic weapon that spat bullets faster than a slot machine paying out in Vegas.

They were outmatched and Andrew doubted they had more ammo than his boss either, so it was only a matter of time before Martin got the advantage he needed.

When they were just a few feet apart, the gun battle going on around them stopped and something hard and heavy slammed into Andrew from behind, driving him down to the floor. Andrew gasped at the fiery pain engulfing him from his bullet wound. Someone cried out and he realized it was a person on top of him.

"Drew!"

Kicking out, he felt the blows connect and the person holding him down eased their grip. It wasn't much but it was enough and he managed to scramble out from underneath his assailant.

Teddy had closed the distance between them and pulled Andrew up. He took a few deep breaths and the panic started to fade but his heart didn't slow from the fast pounding. Adrenaline still flooded his body, making him twitchy and jumpy.

"It's okay, Drew," Teddy said. Or at least that's what it looked like he'd said.

The room erupted into utter chaos. Bullets knocked the lights out, scattering glass everywhere and the walls looked like the practice range of a golf course.

Andrew glanced at whoever had held him down and thought he'd see Martin or the firefighter Teddy had fought with. Instead, it was Thurgood. The agent was lying on his side, his eyes closed.

"Shit, he's been shot. Take off your shirt," Teddy ordered.

Even though his ears were still ringing from the gunshots, Andrew could just about make out Teddy's words.

That was when Andrew spotted the rapidly growing red spot. "I can't, my top has already got my blood on it," he answered, taking just Teddy's shirt and bundling it up against the wound.

Teddy stopped what he was doing and gave him a look.

Andrew didn't have to guess what it was for. "You know I'm clean but Thurgood doesn't know that and I don't want any sort of infection transferring from my wound to his. Beside he's kind of an ass, so I doubt he wants to risk catching 'the gay' from me."

"Hey. Thurgood may well be an ass but he saved your life. Martin had a clean shot at your head," Agent Hammer pointed out as he kneeled next to them.

Andrew sucked in a harsh breath as the other man chastised him. Christopher was right, though. Despite Andrew's dislike of the agent, Thurgood had saved his life. As soon as the guy woke up, he was going to have to swallow some humble pie and say thank you.

"Point," he conceded to Agent Hammer. He ripped off his shirt and took Teddy's too when Teddy handed it to him then put pressure on Agent Thurgood's wound.

"Where is Martin?" Teddy asked, not letting go from where he'd asked Andrew to stabilize Thurgood's head and neck to keep the agent still in case the bullet had damaged his spine.

Agent Hammer kneeled next to them but kept his gun in hand, as he answered. "The last team was close enough to lend assistance but he took something. We think it was a poison since he started convulsing. Damn CIA bullshit. He's being transferred under guard to hospital now. We just need to get Thurgood into an ambulance too."

Poison. "Isn't that a little too James Bond?"

Teddy smiled but Agent Hammer just kept checking Agent Thurgood's pulse as Andrew kept trying to slow the bleeding with their shirts.

Men in assault gear with SWAT written on the back of their Kevlar jackets picked Thurgood up and placed him on a stretcher. They raced out of the room with him. When it was just Andrew and Teddy left, Agent Hammer having gone into the hall to call his mysterious superiors, Teddy looked around the room again.

"Stupid question but… Are you okay?"

He wasn't the only one still a little shocked. Or rather, still a little *in* shock.

"Yes. No. To be honest, I don't have a clue. Ask me in the morning." He groaned, shaking his head and immediately regretted it. A war raged between dizziness and nausea but dizziness won and he sank back to the floor.

"Do you need to go to hospital, Andrew?" Agent Hammer asked. "Genie will kill me if you've been shot again."

"He's fine, Agent Hammer. We'll head over to his sister's house when you're done with us," Teddy stated. "I assume you need to debrief us or some such?"

Thank God Teddy was on the ball. All Andrew wanted to do was curl up and feel sorry for himself for a little while. Now that Martin wasn't out there trying to kill him the relief was starting to mess with his head. But he was still annoyed he'd been played. Andrew *knew* there was nothing wrong with his damn program but Martin had still tricked him.

"That would be the case if we were a branch of the government, Mr Goldbloom. We have everything here covered, so you are both free to go," Agent Hammer said with a secretive smile. His body language completely changed and the man went from cool and calm to uneasy.

"One thing, Mr Finley. Martin turned on your sister, Angela, when she started to run as our armed assault team showed up. He shot her in the head. I'm sorry to tell you she's dead."

Andrew didn't have any reaction to the news other than blinking stupidly. Angela was dead? Andrew had no idea how he felt about that, whether he felt anything at all. Shouldn't he feel something? He tried to sort his thoughts as he tuned out Teddy and Agent Hammer talking. Andrew didn't hear what they said but suddenly Teddy was steering him out of the room.

They maneuvered past the wreckage and the fire chief, who was lying in wait for them on the stairs. Again, he didn't hear anything.

There must have been a portion of time that he blacked out. He heard a car door open and he realized they were in Agent Hammer's car and outside Sara and Steve's house.

His sister and his friend were on the doorstep of their small two-bedroom home. Steve had his arm around her as she cried. At the back of his mind, Andrew thought about how they'd need to build onto it to make it bigger if the fertility treatments were successful and if they decided to adopt as well.

Perhaps he could buy the land behind them.

Teddy asked him a question but the words didn't sink in. So he just shrugged and got out of the car. When his lover came around to his side, he grasped Teddy's hand as if it were a lifesaver. The sheer relief on Teddy's face made him feel like shit.

Somehow he'd forgotten he wasn't the only one dealing with this. But he was the only one having a mini breakdown. Teddy was a firefighter, who was used to dealing with high-stress situations and his body was attuned to the highs and lows of adrenaline. Andrew was a computer geek and spent most of his time looking at a screen, not running about risking his life.

He wanted to kick himself in the ass. This was all happening because of him and instead of holding Teddy close, he'd been pushing the man away. It was a bit wobbly but he managed a small smile as he looked up at him.

Andrew jumped up on his toes and grabbed Teddy down for a hard kiss. He tried to express how grateful he was that Teddy was there, how scared he'd been. Most importantly, how much he cared for Teddy in that one kiss.

Teddy didn't react and Andrew had an irrational moment of fear he was just going to be dumped and abandoned there. He leaped at Teddy and wrapped his arms around Teddy's neck and his legs around Teddy's waist.

It would take a crowbar to pry Andrew off and Teddy couldn't leave if Andrew wouldn't let go.

"Please don't leave me," he whimpered, hating that he was being clingy. Literally. But right now, the stress of everything was catching up and overriding his normal control over his neediness.

"Do you really think that I'll leave you now? *Now?* We've told each other secrets—you mostly escaped a burning building, dodged bullets, both of us have gotten shot, I've risked my job and *now* is when you think I'll leave you?"

Andrew was about to ask what the fire chief had mentioned to Teddy on their way out but then the rest of what Teddy had said sank in. "What the hell do you mean *both* gotten shot?"

"It's only my arm, so I'm fine. One of the ambulance people stuck a padded patch on it when you were given a painkiller. Stop fussing," Teddy advised, shrugging like it was nothing.

To him, getting shot was a big damn deal. But apparently to everyone else, it was like receiving a gnat bite. "Are you insane? You were *shot!*"

Teddy just kissed his nose. "I'm fine."

"You better be fine," he huffed. As soon as they were inside, he was checking every inch of his man. His man. That sounded nice.

"If you're done molesting my brother can you both come in the house so I can hug you and shout at you for getting yourselves in so much damn trouble!" Sara called from the porch.

Teddy kissed his cheek then walked them toward the house. When they got to the steps, Andrew slid down to his feet. He did have some dignity left.

"It was his fault. All of it. Troublemaker," Teddy teased, pointing at him.

Well it's good to know where the man drew the line and ran for cover. For a big man Teddy could run fast too. His lover was up the steps and into the house, dodging around Steve before Andrew could even take a swing at him. Andrew couldn't believe Teddy had actually run away. They were *so* having words later.

But then Steve followed suit, quickly hiding in the house.

"Amazing, isn't it?"

The question from Sara surprised him. "What do you mean?"

"How fast they can run when they want to." She giggled.

He laughed along with her as he thought about watching the two big men beating feet into the house.

But they both sobered fast and settled into an awkward silence.

She looked him over and he could tell she was filing all the scuffs and scratches away for later. Her hair was a mess and she had red, puffy eyes so he guessed she'd already heard the news.

Coughing, he shuffled and didn't meet her gaze. "You know?"

She didn't answer, just nodded and bit her lip. "She wasn't always so awful and I'll mourn the little sister who I used to play dolls with but the monstrous bitch she became won't get a single tear from me," she said with conviction, jutting her chin out stubbornly.

It had been a while since he'd seen that look but from experience, he knew she wouldn't budge. Just like the time she'd stayed quiet a whole three days with a broken finger because her boyfriend at the time had made a joke that girls couldn't punch but they sure could take a few.

So naturally, she'd broken the bastard's nose right there in the middle of the mall. And it was one of the only times he remembered his father laughing so much he'd spat coffee all of over the kitchen table.

They'd all had pizza and ice cream that night. And the guy hadn't darkened their doorway again and none of the local girls gave him the time of day either. Sara always did have a temper.

"Stop smiling at me like that, it's creepy." Sara poked him in the ribs then immediately looked repentant when he cursed and winced.

"Sorry! Come on inside. We set up the spare for you. I assume you and Teddy will be sharing? Steve said he put some *stuff* in there. Does that mean you finally got your cherry popped?"

God help him from inappropriately helpful family interference.

"Please don't ever—*ever*—say that again," he begged, shuddering at the thought of discussing his sex life, now that he had one, with his sister.

They moved into the house and he walked toward the stairs. He'd never been here but he had looked up the blueprints when his sister and Steve had put an offer in on the house.

Sara laughed and rubbed her hands together evilly. "But I'm having so much fun. Did Theo top? Am I using that term right? Top means he fu—"

He slapped a hand over her mouth before she scarred them both for life.

He should have known that wouldn't have stopped her, though. She licked his hand and giggled when he wiped it on her top. Disgusting.

"Eww. Girl cooties."

This time he dodged the finger aiming for his ribs and made a run for the stairs. When he got to the top, he saw Steve and Teddy hugging. It was pretty hot. Seeing them in an embrace, no matter how platonic, distracted him enough that his sister caught up to him.

"Break it up, you two." Sara laughed when she spotted the look on his face. "All this excitement isn't good for Andrew. Now off to bed with you."

Her mom voice did the trick and everyone marched off to do as told.

She is going to make a good mommy.

Teddy knocked him out of his thoughts by pulling the borrowed dusty shirt over his head and wandering into what he presumed was the spare bedroom. He glanced back at his sister and her fiancé to see them in their doorway, smirking knowingly.

"Uh, bye," he stuttered out before following after his lover.

He'd follow Teddy anywhere. But shirtless Andrew would happily walk over hot coals to keep watching the tensing, contracting back muscles and the little dimple at the bottom of Teddy's spine.

And that ass was truly the work of a horny god with miracle hands.

The door shut behind Andrew, startling him, and the thrum of anticipation began to build.

"Take your clothes off and stand by the bed. No—don't turn around," Teddy's voice came from behind him.

Andrew's breathing hitched and his dick hardened. But he did what he was told. When he was naked and standing at the foot of the bed, his back to his lover, he could barely contain his lusty excitement.

His muscles twitched and jumped randomly and he tried to concentrate on the pattern of the metal headboard. Hands ghosted over Andrew's back, making him jump then moan as they pressed harder into his tight muscles. That last painkiller shot was awesome because he didn't feel anything but pleasure.

"You are trouble. I meant what I said to Agent Hammer. You need a keeper." Teddy moved his hands moved over Andrew's back, tracing where he knew the bruises and scrapes surrounded the bullet wound.

Teddy dragged one big hand over his collarbone before moving up his neck. Andrew parted his lips on a ragged breath. Teddy traced the line of Andrew's chin then higher to rub over his lips.

Swallowing the lump in his throat, Andrew tried to gather enough wits to form a sentence. "A-are you applying for the position?" His lips were dry and he licked them, tasting the tip of Teddy's thumb in the process.

"Yes. Do you want me to show you how well I can take care of you? Love you so you'll never even look at another man again?"

There was only one answer. "Yes, please."

Teddy hesitated. "You sure?"

Shivering from anticipation, he shouted his frustration. "Yes!"

"Good," Teddy whispered in his ear, pressing them together, back to chest.

Teddy rubbed his thumb one last time over Andrew's bottom lip as if loath to leave it then lifted away. One hand now lay on Andrew's waist and the other Teddy slid down over Andrew's hip to stop at his thigh.

A tap let him know Teddy wanted him to lift his leg. Teddy raised it until Andrew's foot was on the mattress. The bed was fairly low, one of those trendy futon type things. The warmth at his back disappeared and Teddy stepped away from him.

Before Andrew could ask where he was going Teddy's head appeared through the gap between his legs. Holy shit that was the single most erotic thing he'd ever seen.

He didn't know where to put his hands but that wasn't a problem for long as Teddy grabbed them and gently guided them behind Andrew's back. And he kept them there when Teddy let go and rested a hand on his stomach.

With his other hand, Teddy took hold of Andrew's erection. His arousal skyrocketed and he was close to begging for Teddy to take pity on him. It was embarrassing how near he was to losing it already and he'd barely been touched.

Teddy pumped him a few times then pointed his erection down. He didn't know what his lover was doing until Teddy aimed the tip of his dick and licked the slit.

"Holy shit!"

Watching his dick disappear all the way into Teddy's mouth was amazing. Would he ever be able to do this for his lover? Andrew knew he was fairly large for his size but everything about Teddy was bigger. *Everything*.

He'd managed to take Teddy into his mouth before but at this angle it must be so much deeper and he'd have less control. Well, *he* would anyway. Teddy seemed completely in control.

Teddy sucked his cock, swallowing and making him curl up onto his toes and his balls to tighten to the point of pain. This was going to be over too quickly. Seeing the blue eyes Andrew had dreamed about staring up at him with soft emotion was just too much and he came undone. This was so much better than his teenage dreams.

Just as the first wave of orgasm raced through Andrew's system, Teddy's lips tightened around Andrew's cock, the threat of teeth cutting off the climax before it took hold. "No!"

His hands were released and suddenly he was airborne and falling backwards.

Any anger he felt at being denied his orgasm vanished as he clutched at his lover. Teddy stood but didn't release his waist or his cock so Andrew was taken up too. One of his legs lay over Teddy's shoulder and his other leg under Teddy's other arm, as he clung to Teddy's chest.

"What the hell? Teddy I'm going to fall!" The position pulled at his back but even the slight panic and pain wasn't enough to quell the pleasure and excitement burning inside him.

With a full mouth, Teddy couldn't answer but the look Andrew received clearly said don't be so stupid. Well, excuse him for not wanting to land on his head.

His core muscles were strong but not enough to keep him in this position for long and after a minute, he had to lean back as his abs started trembling violently. The move put him upside down and even though the blood was rushing to his head, Teddy's manipulation kept him hard. He wasn't the only one aroused either. Teddy's huge cock looked even bigger out of the corner of his eye.

It wasn't the best angle but he managed to let go of where he had a death grip on Teddy's leg and take the bobbing shaft into his hand, giving it a few experimental pumps.

He couldn't get a lot of leverage, since he was effectively having to reach behind his neck to touch the base of Teddy's erection. But it was enough. It was more comfortable when he relaxed and he had more control over his strokes too.

He had to trust Teddy completely not to drop him.

This was obviously what Teddy was waiting for, as the second he relaxed Teddy resumed sucking his cock.

In hindsight, gymnastic sex should have waited until they were both healed but damn if he was going bring it up now. He'd deal with the pain later but right now, he wasn't feeling anything but hungry desire.

The sensation was unbelievable. When he gave in and just let Teddy do what he wanted, it got even better. Teddy tightened his lips around Andrew's cock, reminding him who had the power and Andrew shook with pleasure.

"Oh, damn," he panted.

Teddy released Andrew's cock for a moment. Andrew didn't know why until he felt a wet finger probe his hole. He jumped when Teddy captured his cock again. Every part of him loved being pressed up against Teddy but he'd never read about or seen this position before in his long hours browsing the Internet to tackle periods of horny loneliness, so he didn't know what was expected of him.

Teddy did something with his tongue that made Andrew's whole body do the Harlem shake. And he realized that perhaps he was over thinking everything.

A finger eased inside him and back out again, rimming his hole before sinking back in at the same time Teddy's throat contracted around him. Holy Mother of God and space monkeys that felt *so* good.

He was upside fucking down and Teddy seemed bent on sucking his brain out through his cock. Teddy swallowed Andrew's dick once, twice and a third time before the finger inside Andrew suddenly increased to three then he was coming. This time there wasn't anything in the world that could have stopped him from reaching the finish line.

There was just enough time for him to give Teddy's erection one last tight stroke and squeeze before Andrew lost all concept of anything outside his own pleasure. It felt like a never-ending stream of cum erupting from him but Teddy never stopped swallowing it down.

Andrew's eyes were open but he couldn't see anything but stars.

When he came down from the high, he knew he wasn't helping keep himself up at all, he was just hanging limply, draped over Teddy's body. His hands hung above his head and were still miles from the floor.

A slight breeze came through the room, forcing him to shiver. It also made him realize there was something sticky on his neck. Languidly, he wiped at the patch with his hand. Bringing the hand in front of him, he saw a white gooey substance. What—*oh*.

For some reason, possibly the blood rushing to his head, Andrew found that hysterically funny. "You came on my neck," he panted out between breaths and giggles.

"Yep," Teddy panted roughly too, sounding like he'd run a marathon.

Now that the endorphins were floating back under control, he didn't like the feeling of dangling in the air and he stretched down in attempts to put his hands on the floor and dismount his lover like an Olympic class gymnast.

Clearly he wasn't the smart one in this relationship.

"What are you trying to do, Drew?"

"Stand on my hands," he said like it should be obvious.

Silence followed his answer then Teddy tightened his arm around Andrew's waist and the world swirled until Andrew was upright again and gently put on his feet.

He flung his arms out and let himself fall backward. Luckily, the bed was right behind him and he bounced on the mattress instead of the hardwood floor. But he was too tired to care either way.

There just weren't enough positive words to describe how he was feeling right now but if the sex got any better, Teddy was going to kill him with a smile on his face.

"That. Was. Awesome," he wheezed, completely and utterly exhausted.

All Teddy did was laugh before joining him on the bed and pulling him close.

Epilogue

One month later — Teddy

"I'm bringing the last box in now," Teddy called, trying to keep calm.

The pack of Finleys had been unleashed and they were driving him mad. Who would have thought moving one person's stuff would be so difficult.

Of course, it didn't help that he and Drew were still fixing up the house.

They'd had their first argument as a couple the day his chief had said his house was ready for repairs. The structure was still sound but the inside had to be gutted.

Drew wanted to pay for it all to be done right away and Teddy didn't want to take any of Drew's money. He smiled as he thought about the first few times he'd introduced Drew as his lover or his boyfriend.

Drew had gone all pink and started messing with his glasses. It bordered on adorable but Teddy liked his balls where they were so he never said it aloud.

In his head, now that Drew was moving in, they were partners but Teddy knew Drew would need a bit more time to get used to the commitment. So he'd stick with lover or boyfriend and maybe slip partner in every now and again until Drew was used to it.

Drew's family, on the other hand, had no such hesitation. To them, he and Drew were as good as married. The second it became legal in their state, Teddy was popping the question.

Accusations of being a 'macho ass' during their argument about finances, still smarted a bit. And there was just the tiniest bit of his self-esteem that disliked the fact that he couldn't provide for Drew, so maybe Drew was right.

It had taken a while but he'd managed to get Drew to understand that a real home wasn't one he paid someone else to come and do for them, it was one he put sweat and tears into.

In the end, they'd come to a compromise. Drew would pay for everything to get the house back to the point where it had been before the fire, plus a computer room, then they'd fix up the rest together.

Drew had a lot of his sister's stubbornness in him.

Mr Finley, Drew's dad, had received the 'all clear' from the doctors, his own and the one Drew had insisted his father see for a second opinion to make sure.

That was another thing. Teddy was learning Drew was a control freak, everything had to be neat and in the right place. But Teddy was laid-back so he guessed they fit together nicely in that way too. And it didn't take much to make Drew relinquish control if Drew was getting too stressed out.

The funny thing was that after Sara had hit Angela, the family thought Sara was the most dangerous. Or maybe even Angela. But the real danger was Drew. Once the shy man cared about you, he'd always do his best to give you everything you wanted.

Drew had come clean—reluctantly—about how far he'd meddled with his family's lives. His lover had a cute devious side that he was a little scared of. But he'd agreed to back off a little after some...persuasion from Teddy. Teddy smiled as he thought of how adventurous they'd been the night Drew's former CIA employer came after them. They hadn't slept at all that night. Adrenaline was a wonderful thing. And he and Drew had taken full advantage of it. It was the best night of his life.

Teddy still had trouble reconciling the horrible person he knew Angela to be with the girl he hung out with at school.

"Well, hurry up. You think with all those muscles you could move faster than that." Drew smirked, his eyes shining as he looked Teddy up and down.

Seeing Drew hot for him was the single greatest turn on ever.

He needed to be built for his job but that Drew liked that the muscles made it easier for him to keep up his training. He'd even gotten a little pumped up in the last few weeks just to see what Drew's reaction would be.

Sometimes Drew would come down to the station and watch him work out. Teddy could see him gradually growing hornier and hornier until Teddy would have to drive them both home for an early lunch. Teddy already had plans in process for a home gym.

He put the box down slowly and looked at his lover, licking his lips and rubbing a hand over his abs, grinning when Drew tracked the move. Leaping over the box, he swept Drew up into his arms and hoisted him over his shoulder. "How's that for fast?"

"Ha! Put me down you overgrown child!"

"Nope," he refused with a smile at Sara and Genie, who'd come out to see what all the noise was about. He swatted Drew on the butt.

"Come on, you two. You'll have time play with each other later," Drew's mother said as she stepped out onto the porch as well.

Everyone burst out laughing but she just looked confused and no one seemed in a rush to explain why it was so funny.

Without putting Drew down, he crouched to pick up the box again before carrying it into the house. This box wasn't actually Drew's in the strictest sense. But it was *for* Drew, though so he wasn't letting it out of his sight or letting anyone dig through it.

He hadn't forgotten Drew's slip when he'd mentioned his uniform nor had he missed the longing looks Drew wore whenever he'd dropped into the station. So Teddy had managed to sneak his uniform out without anyone noticing.

As long as he could get it back tomorrow, he wouldn't get into any trouble. And most of the team had taken their uniforms home a time or two so now it was his turn.

After he dropped the box off in their room, he finally put Drew on his feet, stealing a kiss before and tugging on a brown ringlet that Drew had grown out for him. He dodged Drew swatting at him.

"You better run." Drew laughed as he raced to the kitchen and hid behind a giggling Sara.

"You going to keep up this time?"

The day after the fire and the shootout with Martin, Agent Hammer had told them Martin had had two plans. The first had been to make it look like the tracking hadn't worked, because he knew that's what Drew would do. The backup plan had apparently been for them to eat the food that traitor Doug had brought them. The lab analysis found the same poison Martin had ingested in all the food in the bags. Martin hadn't died much to Teddy's disappointment. But he wouldn't be going free any time soon so that was something.

Drew skidded to a halt and glared at him. "Don't hide behind my sister. Take your spanking like a man" he goaded.

"Son, I'm glad you're finally happy but I really don't want to know what you and Theodore get up to behind closed doors," Drew's father announced as he walked through the back door.

"Sorry, Dad." Drew's face turned red.

He was so damn cute. The two Finley men had worked out many of their issues although there was still a ways to go. But there was hope.

Teddy looked at Sara when she elbowed him in the side and noticed there was something different about her. "How are you, beautiful?"

"I'm good thanks. Doctor Peters is hopeful the first treatment will work but we won't know for a few weeks yet," she said.

It was clear just how much she wanted the news to be good. Hell, they all did.

It was too early to say but he knew Steve had a good feeling about it. His friend hadn't stopping smiling all week. Now if only they could find Genie a man or woman they'd all be happy.

The wedding had gone off without a hitch and Drew had admitted he'd hacked the adoption list and bumped their application up the line a little. That had led to his and Drew's second fight. Teddy hadn't really agreed with interfering like that since there were so many people waiting on the list, desperate for children to love, but Drew said he'd only shaved off a few months of waiting for the initial interview.

Apparently one or two on the list had some dodgy stuff in their computer history, recent and old, so Drew had knocked them down to the bottom and flagged them as 'to watch' on the children's services database. Teddy realized that it might not have been a joke when he'd said Drew needed a keeper.

"We'll keep our fingers crossed for you." He held out a hand for Drew, loving that his lover came right to him and cuddled up. Teddy didn't have a family so he felt privileged to have been adopted by Sara and Genie as their brother

He leaned down and pressed a kiss to the top of Drew's head. "I love you," he whispered.

"Love you too, Teddy," Drew answered, squeezing him tightly.

About the Author

I'm SA Welsh and I write because the voices in my head keep making me. I love reading and I love letting the characters and stories in my head come to life in a book. I can't function in the morning without a cup of tea and when I'm not writing I'm reading. I have enough books to last me through an apocalypse but don't ask me to share them unless you are a fellow book worm and know how to treat and appreciate a good book. It is thanks to the writers that inspired me to put myself out there that I became an author and the editors that make sense of my chaos that I keep writing.

SA Welsh loves to hear from readers. You can find her contact information, website details and author profile page at http://www.totallybound.com.

Totally Bound Publishing